THE DIAMOND CAT

THE
DIAMOND CAT

Marian Babson

St. Martin's Press
New York

Library of Congress Cataloging-in-Publication Data

Babson, Marian.
The diamond cat / Marian Babson.
p.   cm.
"A Thomas Dunne book."
ISBN 0-312-13049-X (hardcover)
I. Title.
PS3552.A25D5   1995
813'.54—dc20   95-2824   CIP

First published in Great Britain by HarperCollins*Publishers*

First U.S. Edition: August 1995
10   9   8   7   6   5   4   3   2   1

THE DIAMOND CAT

CHAPTER 1

After her first few sleepy blinks, the clock on the bedside table came into focus, registering the time in an evil glow: 2.00 a.m. and the end of sleep. Also the end of peace and quiet.

Outside, a gusting wind shook the windows, hurling rain and hail against the panes. The noise level, she realized, had been slowly rising for some time, disturbing her sleep long before actually waking her. The storm alone could not be blamed for that.

Downstairs in the house shrieks, howls and a desperate keening combined to give the impression that a massacre had started.

'Bettina! Bettina!' Her mother's voice rose over the din, caterwauling with the best of them. 'Get down there and stop all that noise! I told you this would happen! I warned you . . .'

'Yes, Mother.' Wearily, Bettina dragged herself out of bed, closing her ears to the recriminations. 'Don't worry. I'll take care of it. Go back to sleep.'

'Chance would be a fine thing!' her mother retorted with some justice. The sounds of impending battle were ear-splitting. 'Are you sure they can't get out of those cages?'

'They're all right,' Bettina said, with more certainty than she felt. 'The storm is upsetting them, that's all.'

'Never mind *them*,' her mother complained. 'I haven't slept a wink for the past hour. I thought the roof was coming off. And what was that awful thud at the back by the kitchen door? It sounded like half a tree hitting the house.'

'It was probably that drooping bough from Mrs Cassidy's apple tree. It hasn't been looking too healthy lately.'

'Just waiting for a puff of wind to blow it away.' Her mother leaped upon the suggestion. 'I warned May Cassidy. I told her—'

'That's right,' Bettina said absently, closing her mother's door as she went past. The half-remembered after-echo of the thudding sound came back to her. It must have been what wakened her – and started the cats off. They probably thought someone was trying to get in – perhaps their owners coming back for them. Unfortunately, it was impossible to explain Bank Holiday weekends to a cat.

The noise level rose as she reached the foot of the stairs; the yowls turned more urgent and demanding as she went along the hallway, peaking to crescendo as she opened the door and stepped into the kitchen.

'All right, all right,' she soothed, snapping on the light. 'Take it easy now.' A swift glance at the indignant little faces pushed against the bars of their carrying cases assured her that all were present and accounted for. No one had fought their way free with mad intent to destroy the kitchen and each other – it just sounded that way.

Four pairs of eyes blinked against the sudden light and stared at her hopefully. Someone started to purr.

It wasn't Mrs Cassidy's Adolf. He glowered at her unforgivingly, the patch of black fur running from one ear down to his cheek gave him a lopsided, faintly mad look, especially when his green eye glared out from it, in contrast to the yellow eye on the white side of his face. His ancestors had probably started out as odd-eyed whites, but someone in the more recent past had had an interlude with a black tom. Adolf twitched the black moustache above his upper lip and renewed his demands for freedom, more territory and the right to do exactly as he pleased.

The other cats appeared to consider this for a moment, then weighed in with demands of their own.

'Oh, you're well named, Adolf! You're a right little rabble-rouser, you are!' She crossed to the bag of cat treats on the shelf above the kitchen table, considering the alternative of letting them out of their carriers to roam around the kitchen for a bit and, with any luck, wear themselves out enough to go back to sleep. Not much chance of that, though, they were all bright-eyed and alert, obviously ready to begin a long, busy day.

And in fine voice – although it was all sound and fury. If she let them out, they would mingle happily. They all knew each other and played together in the back gardens. They were just in their carrying cases for convenience, so that they wouldn't roam through the house all night, perhaps disturbing things and certainly upsetting her mother.

'Here . . .' She quickly dropped several of the little munchies into each carrier, then stood back with a sigh of relief as the yowls turned to crunching noises.

'Bettina! Bettina!' Unfortunately, the silence meant that she could now hear her mother calling again.

'It's all right.' Bettina went over to the doorway and called back, 'They're quiet now.'

Adolf immediately made a liar out of her. His indignant yowl rose higher than ever. He had never liked her mother's shrill voice; it offended his delicate ears. Bettina looked over her shoulder to see him flick those ears and hurl further imprecations at the source of his discomfort.

'They don't sound it! I'll never get back to sleep now. You might as well make me a cup of tea while you're up.'

'Yes, Mother.' Adolf had set the others off again. She closed the kitchen door and surrendered. Otherwise, they would nag at her all the while she was making the tea.

'All right, all right.' He didn't deserve it but, for the sake of peace, she let Adolf out first. He leaped free and stared around with satisfaction.

'Come on, Pasha.' Sylvia Martin's large ginger Persian was the next most vociferous. He looked, Bettina always thought, more like a feline version of Henry VIII than a pasha, but there was no accounting for the way fond owners saw their cats. Pasha strolled out and shook himself with a benign and lordly air.

'You, too, Enza.' Mr Rawson's dainty little tabby yawned delicately and stretched, quite as though she hadn't been agitating with the rest of them, then sat down in her carrier.

'Do as you please – you will anyway.' Enza was the independent type and entrances fascinated her. She had appeared unexpectedly in Mr Rawson's life, a bedraggled little waif, and taken him over, soon after his wife had died. The story of her arrival and naming was a source of endless enjoyment to Jack Rawson. 'I opened the window and – influenza!' Mr Rawson was fond of chortling. 'In flew Enza!'

Bluebell was waiting patiently. Her bright blue eyes followed Bettina's every move; her purr grew louder. Bluebell belonged to Zoe Rome, who lived next door, and, since the Romes and the Bilbys were close friends as well as neighbours, the little Balinese was in the Bilby house often; she was quite at home there. She was Bluebell not just for her blue eyes but because her movements were so graceful that she seemed to dance rather than walk.

All the cats were out of their carriers now and converging at the back door. They looked at her, then at the door, then back at her.

'You can't mean it,' she said. 'Not in this storm!'

Adolf briefly informed her that he was losing patience with her. He turned and pawed at the foot of the door, his claws making little scrabbling noises as he tried to dig his way under. He seemed quite frantic about something.

'I'm sorry.' Bettina turned away firmly and put the kettle on. 'You'll just have to use the litter box. I'm not letting you out in this. If this wind didn't blow you away, you'd be startled by a burst of hail or thunder and you'd run off and I'm not chasing you all over the neighbourhood in this weather.'

Bluebell appeared to see the justice of this argument and went to sit beside the refrigerator door instead.

A fresh gust of wind slammed against the back door, shaking it on its hinges, blasting it with hailstones that sounded like shotgun pellets.

Enza, too, seemed to have second thoughts and went to join Bluebell by the fridge.

'That's better,' Bettina said. 'It's practically a hurricane out there. You want to stay in where it's nice and warm.'

Pasha wasn't so sure and Adolf definitely wanted to go out. His moustache twitched as he yowled his fury at being thwarted. He clawed frantically at the wood-and-felt strip that kept the cold draughts from penetrating the crack under the door.

'Leave that alone!' Bettina feinted a cuff at him. 'We don't want it clawed off tonight of all nights. It's cold enough as it is.'

Another blast of wind and hail reinforced her words. Pasha backed away uneasily; there was more out there than he wanted to take on.

'Eeeee-rreooow!' Adolf was ready to take on the world. Alone and unaided, he would battle the elements.

Pasha gave him a disdainful look and strolled over to join the ladies; they obviously had the best idea. He sniffed noses with them, then turned and gave Bettina a soulful look. Butter wouldn't melt in his mouth, but he thought it ought to be given the chance to try.

'Bettina!' the accusing voice shouted down the stairs. 'Where's that tea?'

'Kettle's just boiling, Mother. You stay right there. I'll bring it up.' The kitchen was full enough; her mother would make one too many.

'It should have been ready ages ago. You've been messing about with those cats again. You think more of those cats than you do of me.'

'And vice versa,' Bettina Bilby muttered under her breath, in a rare moment of rebellion. A lifetime of living at home and dancing to her mother's wishes had not led to her being any more appreciated. Sometimes it upset her more than others and this was getting to be one of those times. She wasn't even allowed to have a cat of her own – and now that that nasty, snuffly little pug dog of Mother's had gone to the great kennel in the sky, there was no real reason why she shouldn't. Except that it might take too much of the attention Mother felt was *her* due; she was even jealous of 'The Boarders', the neighbourhood cats Bettina looked after when their owners went away for weekends and holidays.

'Bettina – I'm coming down!'

'No, don't!' But the footsteps were already descending the stairs. Bettina heard the telltale creak of the loose board mid-staircase.

'Hurry – inside!' Bettina snatched leftover lamb pieces from the bowl of scraps in the fridge and hurled them recklessly into the carrying cases. Bluebell and Enza flew in after them; Pasha proceeded at a more stately pace.

'There! I knew those cats had got out! I told you so!' A crash of thunder underlined the words as her mother threw open the door and stood like an avenging angel in the doorway.

Pasha put on a spurt of speed and disappeared into his carrier. Adolf stood his ground and swore at her.

'It's all right,' Bettina said. 'I let them out myself.'

'Whatever did you do that for?'

'They were restless. The storm was frightening them. They needed to get out and walk around a bit. It can't be pleasant to be caged up and not able to get away when you don't understand what all the noise is about.'

'Ridiculous!' Her mother rolled her eyes upwards and sighed deeply. 'You have no sense, Bettina. No sense at all. No wonder everyone takes advantage of you.'

'You ought to know,' Bettina muttered. She tried, with a discreet foot behind his hindquarters, to urge Adolf towards his carrier.

'If he wants to go out, let him!' Mrs Bilby caught her. 'One less cat around this place will be all to the good.

I'll open the door for him myself.' She started forward purposefully.

'No, Mother, you can't.' Bettina blocked her way, catching her arm and leading her to a chair at the kitchen table. 'You know you could never face Mrs Cassidy if anything happened to Adolf.'

'I'd like to try. May Cassidy has no more sense than you have. Putting up with a cat like that! Laughing at it and giving him that awful name.'

'He *is* a tyrant,' Bettina said as Adolf turned away to take another swipe at the closed door.

'Nasty, revolting little monster,' Mrs Bilby said.

Adolf flicked his ears and spat something equally insulting but fortunately untranslatable at her.

'Defiant, too,' Mrs Bilby said. 'I don't know how May Cassidy stands the creature.'

'Mrs Cassidy doesn't mind a bit of independence.' Bettina remembered the subservient canine that used to grovel at her mother's feet, whimpering with disgusting delight at any kind word. Some people required slaves and some didn't. Bettina had always liked Mrs Cassidy, even before she acquired Adolf.

'Would you like a sandwich with it?' She set the teapot and cups and saucers on the table. 'Or a piece of lemon cake? There's some left over.'

'Oh, I don't know. I don't really want anything, but I suppose if I don't force myself I'll have a headache in the morning after all this disturbance. Why don't you just make me a simple omelette and, perhaps, a croissant? That shouldn't be any trouble, once you've got the oven hot; the frozen dough is all ready to be cooked.'

'Yes, Mother.' Bettina restrained a sigh; the proposed menu would take at least another half-hour and she'd hoped to get back to bed before dawn – if they were going to have a dawn today. She turned on the electric oven – it would take fifteen minutes to reach the required temperature – then took the eggs and frozen croissants from the fridge and freezer.

11

Adolf suddenly abandoned his vigil by the back door and came to twine round her ankles. She realized that he might not have seen her tossing lamb scraps into the carriers and palmed a fresh piece, allowing him to get the scent of it as she bent to stroke him.

'I hope you're going to wash your hands after putting them all over that dirty cat.'

'Yes, Mother.' Deftly, Bettina flipped the bit of lamb into Adolf's basket and he disappeared after it. She snicked down the door and the doors of the other carriers before turning to the sink to wash her hands.

Shaking her head, Mrs Bilby poured out two cups of tea. Bettina got down a bowl for the eggs and reached for the salt and pepper. She paused as the storm battered afresh at the house and moved over to the window, pulling the curtain aside.

'There goes part of Mr Rawson's fence,' she reported, just managing to discern the chunk of wood being hurled across the bottom of the garden.

'Good! Perhaps he'll have the whole thing fixed properly now. It's been falling apart for years. I warned him. I told him—'

A monumental crash of thunder drowned out her voice. The room blazed with an eerie light. Then everything went dark and silent.

'Are you all right, Bettina?' Her mother's voice was shaken. 'Come away from that window. You know I've always taught you to keep away from windows when there's lightning about. Bettina? Bettina? What's happened? Bettina? Answer me!'

'I'm all right, Mother.' She was still at the window. 'It must have got a power line. The streetlights are out, too.'

'You see? If those cats weren't in their cages, they'd be prowling around underfoot and we'd be tripping over them in the dark and breaking our legs.'

It might not do the cats any good, either, but Mrs Bilby wasn't prepared to consider that. Bettina heard the clink of cup against saucer; nothing was going to deter her mother from her cup of tea.

At least she didn't have to start cooking now. Her eyes only faintly adjusted to the total lack of light, Bettina half groped her way back to the counter and returned the croissant dough to the freezer and the eggs to the fridge. She left the curtains open so that the room was sporadically lit by the flashes of lightning.

Having done the worst of its damage, the storm seemed to be retreating, but the rain persisted, although not quite so heavily.

'You might as well drink your tea, then we can go back to bed. I don't suppose you know where the candles are?'

'I don't want any tea.' Bettina found the candles and matches in the corner of an overhead cupboard and lit one. Tiny pinpoints of light reflected at the doors of the carriers where interested eyes were following every movement.

'I'll just pour another cup for myself then and take it up with me. If you can put your hand on that cake, I'll have a piece of that, too. Goodness knows when they'll get the electricity repaired and we can have a cup of hot tea again. You really ought to put what's left into a Thermos, so we can have something warm in the morning.'

'I'm sure it will be all right by morning.' Bettina juggled candle and cake, then remembered to turn off the oven.

'Leave the light on, then we can tell when the electricity comes back.' Mrs Bilby took the cake and her tea and started for the stairs.

Bettina followed, holding the candle high to shed the best light. At the top of the stairs, the candlelight caught the answering gleam of a descending drop of water just before it splashed to the carpet.

'The roof's leaking again! You should have got the buckets out as soon as you saw how bad the storm was.'

'I'll see to it now.' Bettina sighed, it had been too much to hope that her mother would not have noticed.

13

'You'd better. If this carpet gets wet, it will be ruined –
and we can't afford a new one.' Her mother held the
candle while Bettina got the buckets and bowl they had
learned they needed to control the drips from the roof.

'There . . .' Bettina placed them strategically, trying not
to look up at the wet patches on the ceiling. She had the
uneasy feeling that they were growing larger. It could only
be a matter of time before the plaster began falling and
then she would have to try to cope with having a new
ceiling put in.

'Move that one to the left a bit more.' Her mother was
saying it just to assert her authority; there was nothing
wrong with the original placement of the bucket.

'Yes, Mother.' Bettina kept the peace. 'Why don't you
sleep late in the morning?' she suggested. It would be
even more peaceful to get the cats and kitchen sorted
out in the morning without a running commentary of
complaints.

'I might do that, we'll see. If the cats don't start making
all that racket and disturbing me again.'

'Disgraceful!' Mrs Bilby said with relish. 'Absolutely scandalous!' The newspaper rustled as she turned the pages for the follow-up to the front-page story. 'It just goes to show you can't trust *anyone!* I always suspected the police force was corrupt!'

'Only a few of them, Mother,' Bettina reproved absently. Her attention was centred on the cats. Feeding them was always tricky when there was more than one in residence. Four bowls, one in each corner of the room, had been filled from the various tins that had been delivered along with the cats. Naturally, after a couple of reassuring mouthfuls of their own food, the cats had begun to prowl around to investigate what the others had been served. At the moment, it was peaceful because they were still sampling each other's breakfasts; the crunch would come when one of them decided to return to his own bowl and found another cat eating from it.

'Taking bribes . . . keeping lost property . . .' Mrs Bilby read out the juiciest snippets. 'Five of them suspended and the rest still under suspicion. Disgraceful! In my young days, you could rely on the police absolutely. Now they're no better than anyone else. Worse, it seems! You've got to watch them every minute.'

Adolf was the one to watch. Having finished most of his own food and sampled Enza's and Bluebell's, he was now stalking Pasha with sinister intent. Pasha was still eating his own breakfast, but it was the little puddle of cod-liver oil in the saucer beside his bowl that was Adolf's real target. That meant trouble: Pasha loved his cod-liver oil.

'*And* "there are allegations"' – Mrs Bilby continued to be absorbed in the local scandal – '"that certain of the policemen have been in league with burglars. When householders asked the police to keep an eye on their premises for the two or three weeks they would be away on holiday or on business, the information was passed to burglars who then removed all valuables at their leisure." That must have been what happened to the Burtons last year. Remember? They came back and found the place cleared out. Paintings, silver, china – even the rugs.'

Pasha raised his head and growled threateningly. Adolf snarled back and edged a little closer.

'And remember when Mrs Hailey found that wallet with three hundred pounds in it and handed it in? She never heard another word about it for months and, when she went to inquire, they told her it had been claimed, but she never got a reward or even a thank-you note from the man who lost it. Now it looks as though they kept it all for themselves and never even tried to find the real owner.'

Pasha hissed, challenging the marauder. Adolf adopted an air of unconcern and sauntered past the disputed territory before turning and beginning to sneak up on the other side. Pasha shifted position to face him again, fur beginning to stand on end. He hissed another challenge.

Bluebell and Enza drew together and sat down a safe distance away to watch the proceedings. Only the slight twitching at the end of their tails betrayed their excited anticipation. Since they were not at the moment in a condition where males fought over their favours, they were prepared to take their thrills where they found them. Two males fighting over food would suit them just as well. Enza made an encouraging noise, blatantly inciting them to violence.

'Those cats aren't going to fight, are they?' Mrs Bilby lifted her feet to the rung of her chair, mindful of her bare ankles. 'I told you there'd be trouble having them all here together. One at a time is more than enough. Put them outside where they can't do any damage, otherwise they'll wreck the kitchen.'

'They can't go out,' Bettina said firmly. 'It's still terribly wet out there and some of those downed power lines may still be live. It's too dangerous for them.'

'It's too dangerous for *me* with them thrashing about in here!'

Morning had dawned with a wet and watery sky streaked by ominous grey clouds. There was a persistent wind noisily threatening to break out of control again; bushes rustled and trees bent and swayed. The electricity had come back on, but without radiating any confidence that it would remain on.

The transistor radio warned of damaged gas pipes, live power cables on the ground, fallen trees blocking roads, and the strong possibility of more rain and wind to come. And that was just the news broadcast.

When the weather forecast came on, the forecasters spent a great deal of time explaining just why this should not have happened; the freak atmospheric conditions responsible for it; the impossibility of predicting it and the unlikelihood that such conditions could ever occur again.

Mrs Bilby pointed out that they had said the same thing several years ago and weren't to be trusted as far as they could be thrown.

The noise level in the kitchen rose abruptly as Adolf feinted towards the bowl and Pasha reared up on his hind legs, lashing out to defend his property. Enza howled a battle cry and even Bluebell sang out encouragement, although it was not certain which one she was rooting for. Adolf ducked his head and dived for the cod-liver oil, managing to tip the saucer and spill the oil in the process.

Enraged, Pasha leaped over his bowl and struck out viciously, swearing at the top of his lungs. Adolf backed far enough to give himself room to charge forward, meeting every imprecation with one of his own. Enza and

Bluebell screamed like hysterical cheer leaders, dancing around the periphery of the field of conflict.

'That does it!' Mrs Bilby hurled herself from her chair and charged across the room, flinging open the back door. 'Out! Out! All of you! Out!'

'Mother – no!' But it was too late. Instantly distracted by the scent of the great outdoors, the cats had abandoned their private hostilities and dashed for freedom.

'There!' Mrs Bilby slammed the door behind them and leaned against it, panting. 'Good riddance! Whatever happens, they've brought it on themselves!'

'You shouldn't have done that,' Bettina said, with precarious control. 'I'm responsible for those cats. If they run away and get lost, I don't know how I'll ever make it up to everybody.'

'Nothing will happen to the cats,' Mrs Bilby said defensively.'No such luck! The worst that could happen would be that no one would ask you to cat-sit again. That would be a blessing.'

There was a brief renewed clamour of hatred, defiance and hysteria from outside . . . and then silence. Deadly silence.

'They're gone.' Bettina's heart both sank and raced, all at the same time. 'They've run off. We'll never see them again.'

She pushed her mother aside and wrenched the door open. The air was clear and fresh, scented with the rain.

All four cats huddled in a circle on the small patio leading down to the garden. There was a large puddle where the cement met the grass, marooning them on the damp cement. The cats were staring intently at something on the ground in front of them. Their tails lashed slowly back and forth, their bodies tensed to spring. They were united against some common enemy.

'Now what have they done?' Mrs Bilby crowded into the doorway behind her.

'I don't know.' Bettina's heart refused to return to its

proper place. There was something about the crouching intensity of the cats that boded no good.

'What have they got there?' Mrs Bilby craned her neck. 'Take it away from them and see.'

'Probably a shrew or a vole.' Bettina approached cautiously, dreading the moment when she would have to stoop and retrieve the small furry body. But it had to be done, the cats would be sick if they ate it.

Four voices rose in protest as her hand came down in their midst, groping for their lawful prey. It was injustice of the highest order. They were used to it, of course, but they didn't have to like it.

Adolf, bolder than the others, slammed a proprietary paw down on his victim and growled. This was his. His alone. He glared at the other cats.

'I think he's got a bird.' Divide and conquer was the method. Bettina scooped up Bluebell, who gave only a token struggle, contriving to wipe her feet on Bettina's sleeve and bursting into purrs; she hated getting her feet wet.

'Here.' Bettina passed Bluebell to her mother. 'Put her inside.' She reached for Pasha, the next most amiable.

But Pasha wasn't going to live up to his reputation today. Some of Adolf's stroppiness was rubbing off on him. He twisted away from her hands and muttered a protest.

'Oh!' She had a clear view now. 'They've got a pigeon.'

'Well, get it away from them before they make themselves sick on it. Nasty creatures! You can't let them out of your sight for a minute, but they run off and kill something. I'll never know why you want them around.'

'I don't think they killed it,' Bettina defended. 'They didn't have time. They just got out here.'

'The poor little pigeon. It probably took one look at all those great louts charging down on it and dropped dead from fright. Mark my words: they killed it – one way or another.'

'Nonsense! It's been dead for hours.' Bettina had taken

a better look at the body now and it was definitely stiff, its head cocked to one side in an unnatural way. 'The storm must have hurled it against the house and broken its neck.'

'A likely story! You're covering up for those cats.'

'That must have been the thud that woke us in the night,' Bettina realized. 'And that was why the cats were so anxious to go outside. They knew – and they wanted to get at it.'

'While it was still fresh!' Her mother sniffed. 'Disgusting monsters! Just like them! As though they didn't get enough to eat with you taking care of them and spoiling them to pieces.'

Adolf twitched his ears, growled menacingly and put another paw on the motionless and rain-drenched body. Pasha moved over to stand beside him, glaring at Bettina and her mother with unusual defiance.

Enza started forward and incautiously stepped into the puddle. She drew back, shaking her paw and complaining. This was no fit weather for cat or human. She withdrew to Mrs Bilby's ankles and looked pointedly at the kitchen door.

'That's right, Enza.' Mrs Bilby was slightly mollified. 'You've got a bit of sense. You and Bluebell. We'll go back inside where it's dry and warm.' Bettina heard the door close behind them.

'Now then . . .' With her mother out of the way, Bettina was prepared to be tougher. 'Let's get that out of your grubby paws.' She swooped and snatched up the dead pigeon.

Adolf shrieked an immediate protest, but Pasha was distracted by the sudden enormous raindrops splashing down on him. The random storm clouds were overhead again and the heavens were about to open once more. Pasha looked skyward then moved back to the shelter of the porch, huddling against the kitchen door.

Adolf was made of sterner stuff. He bristled and snarled his fury. His tail lashed, he advanced menacingly, screaming of Anschluss and Blitz – but he had lost his audience.

Bettina stared down at the pathetic feathered heap in her hand, her heart constricting with dismay. This wasn't just any common wild pigeon, this was – had been – someone's pet. The little tube attached to its leg told her that.

A racing pigeon? A homing pigeon? No, a carrier pigeon. A bird loved and cared for, living in a loft with others of its kind. Heading homewards towards shelter and its mate when it had been blown off course by the sudden storm, its tiny, ordered, happy life unexpectedly and cruelly ended.

It would have had a name, probably a favourite perch in the loft, a feeding tray filled with its favourite grain, a mate – a grieving mate. And an owner who would be watching the sky for its return, hoping against hope that it had found shelter from the storm and would eventually flutter in safe and sound, although much delayed . . .

'Bettina! Bettina!' The kitchen door opened and Pasha immediately hurled himself against it and shouldered his way through. 'Bettina, are you going to stay out there all day? It's raining again.'

'Yes, Mother, I know.' Even Adolf had noticed. The wind was rising and those first large splashing drops were turning into a concentrated downpour. He was no longer willing to stay and assert what he felt to be his rights over the pigeon; his main rights were to a roof over his head and solid creature comfort. He was at the door ahead of her.

'We're coming.' She turned the knob and opened the door, allowing Adolf to streak in ahead of her, confident that he would distract her mother for the few moments she needed.

'That's Pasha's cod-liver oil, you miserable little tyke!' Sure enough, Adolf was running true to form and her mother was attempting to exert her authority; they would both be kept busy for the next few minutes.

Bettina stood on one leg, drawing up the other one to

form a half-lap on which she laid the pigeon while she struggled to remove the message container from the stiff, cold leg. There would be identification inside the tube; someone to notify of the fate of a cherished pet.

Again Bettina felt her heart constrict and flutter as wildly as the little wings must have beat against the storm. She didn't want to be the breaker of such sad news. All this while, she had secretly dreaded the accident which might have forced her to face the owner of one of her charges with such terrible tidings.

Now the nightmare was upon her, lessened only by the anonymity of the owner and the unfamiliarity of the corpse. In a way, that made it even more awkward. How do you telephone a complete stranger and say . . . ? Say . . . ? How *did* you phrase it to break the news in the kindest manner?

'Bettina! Bettina! Are you coming in? The storm's come back and these ruddy cats are running wild in here.'

'Yes, Mother, I'm here.' Bettina slipped the cylinder into the pocket of her cardigan and opened the door. 'Do you have a shoe box or something we can put the pigeon in?'

'You're never bringing that thing in here! Shoe box? Are you out of your mind? Go down and throw it in the ditch where it belongs. You'll be wanting to give it a Christian burial next!'

No . . . but she wanted to save it. Its owner would want to know what had happened to it; he might even want the body back in order to bury it himself. (Pigeon fanciers were usually men, weren't they? Except for Her Majesty the Queen, that is.) Perhaps in some private plot of ground where he interred all his deceased pigeons.

'That's not a bad idea.' She knew her agreement would infuriate her mother, but that was better than letting her know the real reason the pigeon was going to be preserved. She wrapped the little corpse in paper towels and looked around for a place to store it.

'Don't you dare go near the freezer!' her mother snapped. 'I'm not having that thing in there!'

'I'm just going upstairs,' Bettina said. 'I think I have a box it will fit into in my room.'

'All the dead birds and animals there'll be around after this storm,' her mother grumbled, 'and you have to go and get sentimental over one just because it's died on our doorstep.'

Adolf nearly tripped Bettina as she crossed the room; he was still noisily protesting the confiscation of his prize. Pasha trailed after him uncertainly, ready to join in if the pigeon were restored to them, but obviously coming to a more realistic assessment of the situation, for he lost interest abruptly and turned back to finish his cod-liver oil before Adolf remembered it.

Too late. Bluebell and Enza had discovered it and were licking the saucer to a fine polish. Muttering under his breath, Pasha retreated to his carrier, crouched down in front of it and sank into a monumental gloom.

Outside, the rain began to beat down heavily again.

'Typical Bank Holiday,' Mrs Bilby said with deep satisfaction. 'I don't know why anyone tries to go away. At least, not to stay in this country. They ought to have learned better by now. Even you are smart enough not to do that.'

Bettina made an indeterminate noise in her throat, rather like Pasha's complaints. Any attempt she had ever made to get away for a holiday on her own or with friends had inevitably been thwarted by one of her mother's 'attacks', necessitating her cancelling her plans and staying at home to nurse her mother back to 'health'. It had not taken many such episodes before she had learned her lesson.

Pasha gave a querulous moan and Bluebell and Enza abandoned the empty saucer and went over to minister to him, although it was debatable whether breathing the fumes of his own cod-liver oil all over him was going to be any comfort to Pasha.

'Look at the way those cats carry on.' Mrs Bilby watched

23

disapprovingly. 'It's a good thing Pasha is the way he is or there might be trouble there.'

'Poor Pasha,' Bettina defended him. 'He can't help it. I must remember to give him his vitamin pills every day.'

'Sylvia had to refund the last few stud fees when there weren't any results, didn't she?' Mrs Bilby did not attempt to disguise her ill-humoured glee. 'Jack Rawson says his name shouldn't be Pasha, but Eunuch.'

'Jack Rawson had better pay more attention to his own cat.' Bettina glanced at Enza, whose gently burgeoning sides suggested a happy event in the not-too-distant future.

'Irresponsible!' Mrs Bilby glared at Adolf — there was little doubt who was responsible for Enza's predicament. 'They should all be fixed!'

The paper towels were now soaking wet from the water draining off the feathers. Absently, Bettina unwrapped the pigeon, tossed the towels into the waste bin and pulled off fresh towels to shroud the bird.

This sent Adolf into fresh paroxysms. He reared up on his hind legs to bat out with a front paw, trying to hook the bird from her hand. She lifted it higher.

'Yes, I mean you!' Mrs Bilby snapped at Adolf. 'Especially you! You're the troublemaker around here.'

Adolf dropped back to all fours and swore harshly at Mrs Bilby, recognizing animosity and returning it. They were old adversaries and he was not easily going to forget the sudden glasses of cold water hurled over him as he strolled through the garden. He knew who was responsible for them.

'I'll get this out of the way.' Bettina gestured with the bird. 'He won't be so excitable then.'

'That's right, get it out of here. And don't keep it in your room, either. It won't be long before it starts to smell. Bury it, if you're going to, and get it out of the way.'

'I can't bury it now.' The rain was lashing down, a howling gale shook the windows, it was pitch dark again. Perhaps they had just been in the eye of the storm for the past few hours; it seemed to have returned with renewed vengeance. The kitchen had turned dark and claustrophobic.

'Put the light on.' Her mother shivered suddenly. 'This is going to be a dreary day.'

As she snapped on the wall switch, the light flickered ominously before settling down to a steady glow, much dimmer than it should have been.

Bluebell looked at the light bulb, then at the rain-streaked windows, and retreated into her carrier to curl up on her favourite blue velvet cushion. This was going to be a good day to sleep. The others seemed of a mind to agree with her and drifted towards their own soft-cushioned carriers.

'We can't need a new light bulb already,' Mrs Bilby said. 'They must have cut the power.'

'They have a lot of lines down in this storm already,' Bettina said. 'They'll be trying to conserve what power they have. It's better to have weaker power than none at all.'

'You'd best start cooking that chicken now then. It's going to take longer than usual and, if we lose the electricity entirely, we can eat it cold once it's cooked. Boil plenty of potatoes, too, so that we can have potato salad with it.'

Bettina agreed, regretting, not for the first time, that they didn't have a gas stove. This problem didn't seem to occur with gas pipes well underground.

'For heaven's sake, get rid of that thing and wash your hands first!'

'I'm just going to.' Evading Adolf's last-ditch attempt to retrieve his prey, Bettina slipped out of the kitchen and closed the door firmly behind her.

It was dark and gloomy in the hall, the rain drummed relentlessly against the art deco stained-glass window on the landing, threatening to break it with the next gust of wind. It was also chill and dank.

Automatically, Bettina glanced ceilingwards, checking

for new leaks. A steady drip-drip-drip into the buckets reminded her that they needed emptying. So did the two bowls in the corners where a slow trickle of water seeped down from unidentified weaknesses somewhere above.

The roof needed mending. Needed replacement, in fact. But where was the money to come from? Her salary, combined with her mother's pension, just managed to cover the bills they had now. She didn't want to think about the rumours that Jelwyn Accessories was in financial difficulties and perhaps heading for bankruptcy. She had worked there since leaving school, rising from office junior to personal assistant to David Norris, one of the partners. It was the only work she had ever known; it would not be easy to find a new job for someone over forty – even if the country wasn't still struggling out of a recession.

She closed the door of her room behind her firmly; she always did. It gained her those few extra seconds from the moment she heard the creak of the fourth stair from the top and the moment her mother threw open the door without knocking. Just time enough to toss one of the magazines her mother thought too expensive or one of the novels her mother considered too risqué (it didn't take much – there weren't many novels Mrs Bilby approved of these days) into one of the drawers or under the bed.

Inside, she leaned against the door and looked around indecisively. The tiny burden in her hand seemed to have gained weight and become cumbersome. It was sheer imagination to think that a whiff of faint corruption was already rising from it.

But she did not want to set it down on top of the dressing table or – heaven forbid! – the bed.

After a moment, she pulled a copy of *Vogue* from the top drawer of the dresser and put it on the windowsill, carefully settling the paper-towel swathed pigeon on top of it.

She stood there for a minute, looking out on the storm. The wind swept wildly across the adjoining gardens of the terraced houses, bending trees and bushes, shaking fences and hedges; torrential rain was turning puddles into ponds. The sky lit briefly, then a rolling crash of thunder shook the window.

Instinctively, Bettina stepped back and pulled the curtains shut. Not before she had seen another bough break away from Mrs Cassidy's apple tree, however, and go tumbling across Jack Rawson's garden, ploughing a furrow through his neat rows of cabbages.

She sat down on the edge of the bed and turned on the lamp on the bedside table – quickly, while they still had electricity. At this rate, the power was going to fail again any moment now.

'Bettina! Bettina!' her mother shouted from the foot of the stairs. 'Are you all right? That lightning was close.'

'Yes, I'm fine,' she called back. 'I'll be right down.'

'Don't bring that thing with you!'

'I wasn't going to.' She didn't really want to keep it in her room, either. She wanted to get rid of it, the sooner the better. If it weren't for the storm, she would put it outside somewhere – but then she'd have to worry about the cats finding it again.

Surely the bird must have been carrying some identification. She took the small cylinder from her pocket and uncapped it. Vaguely, she had expected to find a small scroll of paper inside, perhaps with a message; certainly with the name and address of the owner.

The top of the tube seemed to be blocked with a minute piece of cotton wool. With the tips of her fingernails, she managed to get hold of a fleck of the wool and tugged gently. It had been firmly wedged in but, after a moment, it yielded suddenly. She dropped the wool on the bedside table and raised the tube to eye level, squinting into it in the dim light.

The expected slip of paper was not there. At least, not immediately apparent. There seemed to be another obstacle clogging the cylinder. She prodded the blockage with the tip of her little finger, but nothing happened.

'Bettina! Bettina!' her mother called again.

With an impatient exclamation, she upended the cylinder over the palm of one hand and tapped the end of it with the other. At first there was resistance then, with the abruptness of closely packed olives tumbling out of their bottle, the contents of the cylinder spurted out.

Only they weren't olives.

A shimmering cascade of small objects spilled into her hand, shooting off bright multicoloured sparks even in the dim light. She gasped, staring down at them incredulously.

A tiny heap of gems rested in the palm of her suddenly trembling hand, vibrating and burning with an inner life of their own.

Diamonds!

She was holding a fortune in flawless blue-white diamonds in the palm of her hand.

CHAPTER 3

'BETTINA! BETTINA! Are you coming down? I'm trying to stuff the chicken and these animals are plaguing the life out of me! Get down here and control them!'

'All right! All right! I'm coming!' Frantically, she tried to scoop the diamonds back into the little cylinder, but they wouldn't all fit. They must have been packed in with geometric precision by—

By whom?

She tilted them out again and peered inside, still looking for some scrap of paper to establish the identity of the owner of the bird, of the diamonds. Something, anything . . . but there was nothing. The inside of the tube was whistle-clean and empty. It had contained nothing but the gems.

'BETTINA!'

Immediately upon her mother's shout, Adolf's voice rose in the indignant plaint of a cat who has been most unfairly trodden upon. Or possibly kicked.

'Yes, yes! I'm coming!' She began dropping the diamonds back into the cylinder one at a time. They still weren't all going to fit, tossed in in this haphazard way; there wasn't even going to be room to replace the cotton-wool stopper – and there would still be gems left over.

There was a shriek from downstairs, followed by a crash of crockery and several hysterical yowls.

'BETTINA! If you don't get down here at once, I won't be responsible for what I do to these bloody cats!'

'All *right!*' Three diamonds wouldn't fit in: an emerald cut, a round and a pear shape. They lay on the table beside the cylinder, quietly glittering. She rammed the top of the cylinder in place and looked around wildly for somewhere to hide it. Somewhere her mother would not look. Was there such a place?

Despite her protests, Mrs Bilby regularly entered her room in her absence; suddenly tidied drawers or a pristine carpet and scent of furniture polish silently proclaiming: 'I was only trying to help, dear.' That the help involved poking and prying into every corner was simply unfortunate, but the place had to be kept clean. Long ago, Bettina had learned that it was safer to keep anything personal in her desk at the office, risking the occasional forays of curious cleaners, than to expose it to her mother's ruthless inspection. But it had been a long time since she had had anything she wanted to keep that secret.

'BETTINA!'

'Yes!' She thrust cylinder and loose diamonds into her cardigan pocket, snatching a couple of paper handkerchiefs from the box on the bedside table to ram down on top of them for protection. Getting up, she stamped her feet noisily all the way across the room to signal that she was actually on her way this time. *Damn!* She needed time to think, but that was a luxury she seldom achieved when her mother was around.

'You always did have a temper,' her mother greeted her as she stamped into the kitchen. 'I thought it was getting better, but it isn't. It's all because of those cats, if you ask me. If you didn't have them to worry about, you'd be more reasonable.'

'The cats have nothing to do with it.' Bettina spoke between clenched teeth.

'The cats have everything to do with it. If they hadn't killed that pigeon, you wouldn't be left with a dirty dead bird in your nice clean room and you wouldn't be in such a state. You're not going to leave it there all night, are you?'

'I'll take care of it, you don't have to worry.' She hadn't

thought that far ahead. 'And the cats didn't kill it. It broke its neck hitting the back of the house.'

'So *you* say,' her mother sniffed.

She was never going to hear the last of this, she knew. And her mother didn't know the half of it. If she ever found out about the diamonds . . .

The one with the real temper was her mother. If she hadn't lost it and swept the cats out in a fury, they would never have discovered the dead pigeon and the gales would eventually have blown it away to rest in someone else's yard, where it would be someone else's problem. Or, better still, into the woods nearby, where one more decomposing pigeon wouldn't have been worth a second glance. And no one would ever have found the diamonds.

'I put the chicken into the oven,' her mother said with a martyred air. 'I didn't wait to stuff it, the cats were getting too excited.'

'We can manage without stuffing,' Bettina said absently. Culinary arrangements were the least of her preoccupations at the moment. Except for one other. It was suspiciously quiet in here.

'Where are the cats?' She looked around.

'They're all right.' Her mother's eyes shifted uneasily.

'I didn't ask how they—' She broke off and raised her voice, calling: 'Bluebell . . . Enza . . . Pa—'

Adolf's overriding yowl broke into the roll call. He was furious, he was affronted – and he was outside.

'Oh, no!' Bettina dashed for the back door and threw it open. Three cats in various stages of bedragglement scurried into the kitchen. 'Oh, Mother! How could you?'

'I told you to come down. They were driving me crazy. I warned you I wouldn't be responsible—'

'They'll catch their deaths of cold!' Bettina captured Pasha, who looked the worst, perhaps because of his long coat now plastered to his skin. She snatched paper towels and began blotting him. Enza and Adolf began weaving around her ankles, leaving wet patches where they rubbed against her. Pasha, Enza and Adolf . . .

31

'Bluebell!' she cried frantically. 'Where's Bluebell?' She leaped to her feet, tumbling Pasha to the floor. 'She's still outside.'

'Bluebell's all right,' her mother said as her hand closed around the doorknob.

'*Prrr-yaaah?*' At the same moment, the triangular little face poked out from the carrying case, eyes blinking.

'Bluebell's a little lady,' Mrs Bilby said. 'She's not a ruffian like those others. She's been asleep in her own little hidey-hole until we decide to feed her. I don't mind Bluebell; she knows her place.'

Adolf sent Mrs Bilby a filthy glare and hissed sharply.

'Not like that nasty defiant mongrel.' Mrs Bilby returned the sentiment.

A faint urgent pain began throbbing its message at the base of Bettina's skull. It was time to take another tranquillizer and hope that the hovering headache did not settle in for the rest of the day.

'You shouldn't have turned them out into the wet.' It was pointless arguing with her mother; Bettina picked up the despondent Pasha and finished drying him as much as possible.

'You know very well you shouldn't have all these cats around. If the proper authorities knew what you were doing, you'd be stopped. There are regulations about how many animals you should be boarding at any one time – and you're way over the limit for the accommodation you can provide. You're acting like a cattery – without any of the licences or permissions you need for that.'

A cattery. For a moment, Bettina was caught up in the impossible dream: a little house with plenty of land, room enough for a row of small heated chalets with their own exercise runs. A procession of legal boarders, paying their way. Perhaps even a cat or two of her very own . . .

'If anyone decided to report you for what you're doing,' Mrs Bilby said darkly, 'you'd be in dead trouble!'

Bettina put Pasha down slowly and gave her mother a long level look, of the sort she rarely permitted herself. It was bad enough that she could never realize her dream, but if she were to be denied the occasional comfort of The Boarders . . .

'If *anyone* reported me,' she said evenly, 'I'd have a pretty good idea who it was – and I'd walk out of this house and you'd never see me again.'

It was more than she had ever said to her mother before and the words shocked them both. But she meant them. The sudden knowledge lay between them like an impassable crevasse.

'Bloody cats!' her mother said. 'Come here, Enza, let me dry you off.' She reached for the more amenable Enza and pulled her into her lap, beginning to stroke the fur with her bare hands before belatedly reaching for a towel. She avoided Bettina's eyes.

'Here, Adolf!' Adolf carried no grudge against Bettina and settled contentedly on her lap.

Bluebell yawned delicately, stretched and sat down in front of her carrier, tucking her long plumed tail neatly around her legs, ready to supervise the domestic activity going on. Pasha went over to her, murmuring complaints deep in his throat, looking for sympathy. Bluebell regarded him solemnly for a moment, then began to wash his face. He stretched out beside her and, after an aggrieved look at the rain lashing against the window-pane, allowed himself to be comforted. They both began to purr.

The lights flickered and resumed their glow at a distinctly lower brightness.

'There,' Mrs Bilby said. 'I hope that oven is hot enough. We'll have to add at least an hour to the cooking time, from the look of this.'

Enza and Adolf were as dry as they were going to get for a while, but showed no inclination to leave their respective sheltering laps. Bluebell and Pasha had gone to sleep, entwined in contentment.

Mrs Bilby sighed deeply and reached for her newspaper again, returning to the iniquities of the local police.

'They're all on suspension – with full pay, I'll wager. That's usually the way it goes. And I suppose they'll be allowed to take early retirement with no loss of pension. You can't trust anyone these days. Even stealing the things turned in to Lost and Found. Just think of it!'

'Just think,' Bettina echoed. She had been thinking of little else since she found the diamonds. There was no guarantee that the new police brought in to replace the suspended officers would be any more honest – if the temptation were strong enough. Working for Jelwyn Accessories, she knew just enough about gems – from their disastrous foray into genuine jewellery, as opposed to costume jewellery (one of the reasons they were in the current financial plight) and rather exotic motor accessories – to know that she was in possession of a substantial fortune.

If she handed it in to the local police, it might be lost for ever. If she went to a police authority farther afield, the problem remained the same, with the added complication that she might not be believed when she tried to explain how she had come into possession of the gems.

If only the pigeon wasn't dead. If it had just been hurt, disorientated – maimed, even – there would have been the possibility of nursing it back to health and sending it on its way again, carrying its awkward cargo to its rightful owner.

Who *was* the rightful owner? The person who had dispatched the diamonds or the person who waited to receive them? And what was any bird doing carrying such a valuable cargo? And not carrying any identification? Why would anyone send a bird out into a storm like this to begin with? What was going on?

No honest – or legal – explanation sprang to mind. Smuggling seemed the obvious explanation. These days, one usually thought of drug smuggling, but the value of the diamonds was well above that of the same cylinder tightly packed with any drug. Had some dishonest entrepreneur in Amsterdam or Brussels launched his bird out over the Channel in an attempt to evade Customs and Excise? That possibility might also explain the bird being aloft in such a storm – the weather might have been quite all right on the Continent. Of course, the intensity of the storm had been unexpected in this country, too. It had ruined someone's carefully laid plans.

'*Bettina!*' Her mother's voice penetrated her thoughts. 'This is the third time I've spoken to you. I don't know where your mind is!'

And may you never find out. 'Sorry, Mother,' she said. 'I'm afraid I'm half asleep. The weather must be making me drowsy.'

'You and the cats!' Mrs Bilby swept a scornful glance over the sleeping felines. 'Sometimes you're just alike.'

'The cats have got the right idea in this weather.' A hopeful thought occurred to her. 'Are you sure you wouldn't like to go upstairs and take a little nap yourself?'

'Certainly not!' Mrs Bilby laughed shrilly and scornfully. Adolf twitched his ears and swore softly. Enza, startled awake, shook her head groggily and leaped to the floor, moving to the far side of the room.

It had been too much to hope for, of course. Mrs Bilby only retired to her room when *she* felt like it.

Enza inspected her food dish, but nothing interesting had been added to it since last she looked. She muttered her opinion of this lack of hospitality and went over to nudge herself into the cosy huddle of Bluebell and Pasha. They grumbled, but shifted lazily to make room for her.

Adolf sat up abruptly, as though sensing he might be missing something. He looked around, raised his head to sniff the delicious aroma of roasting chicken coming from the oven and turned to Bettina expectantly.

'Not yet,' she told him. 'It isn't cooked.'

'Talking to a cat like that!' her mother scoffed. 'As though it could understand what you're saying. You're a fool, Bettina. There's a lot of your father in you.'

Bettina stood up abruptly, sending Adolf leaping to the

35

floor. Suddenly the kitchen was too claustrophobic, too small to hold all the personalities in it.

'I'd better go and empty those buckets.' She kept her voice even. 'Before they get too full to manage.'

'Now you're being sensible,' her mother approved. 'Pay some attention to the things that really matter. I always say—'

Bettina closed the door quietly behind her, discovering that her teeth were clenched so tightly her jaw was beginning to ache. She had known it was going to be a long weekend; she had not realized quite how long it was going to be. She had not made allowances for the storm. No one had. She had never envisioned being trapped inside the house all day, every day, unable to get out as far as the end of the garden.

What would life be like if Jelwyn Accessories closed down? If she were condemned to spend all her time in this cramped little house . . . with her mother? Even if she were able to invent enough errands to keep her outside for most of the day, they would still be spending far too much time together.

Only the cats were going to keep her sane this weekend. What would she do without them?

The buckets were nearly full, she emptied them and replaced them, then did the same with the bowls under the lesser drips. It didn't take long. Rather than return to the kitchen immediately, she went to her room and stood at the window watching the world drowning outside.

The presence of the feathered corpse on the windowsill was curiously disturbing. Unpleasant. She certainly did not want to spend the night with it in her room. Nor did she care for the idea of leaving it propped on the ledge outside the window, even supposing the driving wind and rain wouldn't knock it to the ground and blow it away.

In which case, there would be no evidence that the pigeon had ever reached this house, nothing to connect it with the pocketful of diamonds . . .

She tried to pull her thoughts away from the temptation. How much would the diamonds be worth? And how would one go about selling them? Surely any dealer would want an explanation as to how she came to be in possession of such jewels. Of course, it might be easier to sell them one at a time. But to whom? And how good a price would she get? She was no good at bargaining, she knew, and she vaguely recalled having read that jewel thieves only got a fraction of the true value of the jewels—

She was not a thief! Not even the 'stealing by finding' kind, which this would amount to – if she kept the gems. But what else was she to do with them? What possible chance was there of finding the true owner – and how? Should she advertise in the newspapers? That would surely bring a horde of false claimants.

And who was the true owner? What sort of bird lover would stuff the priceless gems into a carrier pigeon's message cylinder? There had to be a strong suspicion that the gems were criminally acquired and headed for an illegal destination. Perhaps they were the results of a jewel robbery, prised from their settings and en route to someone who would mount them in new settings so that they could be sold as new and innocent pieces.

A fresh burst of rain mixed with hail struck viciously against the window. She looked out at the storm, almost with gratitude. It meant that she literally could do nothing right now. And the Bank Holiday meant that there was no use in trying to reach anyone by telephone, all offices and businesses would be closed. She had time to think and try to decide what to do.

Meanwhile, there was still the pigeon. She found several plastic shopping bags in her closet and wrapped the bird thoroughly before putting it into a shoe box. So far, so good, but she still didn't want it in her room. She had the uneasy feeling that decomposition would still be going on, no matter how well she wrapped it up.

There was nothing for it but the freezer – if she could manage to smuggle the pigeon into it when her mother wasn't looking. Mrs Bilby rarely checked the contents of the freezer, preferring to leave that to Bettina, who could be depended upon to buy anything that was needed to keep it well stocked.

Yes, the freezer should be a safe place to stash the bird until she could decide what to do about everything.

CHAPTER 4

It was a nasty shock to walk into the kitchen and find her mother bending over the open freezer chest.

'I thought I'd better check it.' Mrs Bilby sounded curiously on the defensive; perhaps something in her daughter's attitude told her she was overstepping some invisible line. 'In case the power goes again. They say you're supposed to have it fully packed and, if not, to fill up the space with a blanket or newspapers, so that it will hold the cold better until the power is restored.' There was a pile of newspapers at her feet.

Bluebell was also there. She knew what the freezer was – a fine source of food. Not so good as the fridge – you had to wait for it to be thawed and cooked – but one that gave promise of future delights. She reared up on her hind legs, front paws resting on the edge and arched her neck, straining to look inside.

'Oh, take her away, Bettina.' Mrs Bilby pushed at Bluebell. 'If that lid should fall, she'll lose her paws.'

If the lid fell, it would brain her mother first. The thought brought a faint guilty smile to her face. Quickly, Bettina gathered up Bluebell, who had just given her a better idea of what to do with the pigeon.

'I think I ought to check Zoe's freezer,' she said. 'Just in case. It would be terrible if they came home and found everything ruined.'

'Can't do any harm,' her mother agreed, 'as it's just next door. I hope you're not planning to go chasing all over the neighbourhood to the others though. You'll get soaked and catch your death of cold.'

'Mrs Cassidy and Mr Rawson just have freezer compart-
ments in their fridges,' Bettina said. 'Small ones. They
don't hold enough to make much difference if they thaw
out. Sylvia . . .' She hesitated.

'Sylvia! You don't need to worry about that one! She
has more money than she knows what to do with. You
can tell that by the way she throws it away on nonsense.'
Mrs Bilby sent poor Pasha a malevolent glance. She had
never got over learning how much he had cost. And then
Zoe had had to go and buy the outrageously expensive
Bluebell, lovely though she was, to try to keep up with
the Joneses. It was the terror of her life that Bettina also
might succumb to the general madness and catch the
delusion that she could make money by breeding pedigree
cats.

('He's worth his weight in diamonds!' Sylvia had
burbled persuasively last year, cuddling the year-old Pasha
she had just acquired. 'He's a champion already, top prizes
in every show he's been in. People will be queuing up for
his services, there'll be lots of stud fees. And later, we can
buy him his own little queen or two and breed our own
kittens. Do you know kittens can sell for as much as five
hundred pounds, and up to seven hundred and fifty
pounds?'

('If he's so valuable,' Mrs Bilby had questioned suspiciously, 'why were his owners willing to sell him?'

('Oh, business,' Sylvia had said vaguely. 'They're in
business. They can't keep every cat. They have plenty of
others. But this one is mine now, aren't you, darling?'
She had hugged Pasha. 'My own little gold mine, my
worth-his-weight-in-diamonds cat.')

'I won't be long,' Bettina said. 'I'll just get my raincape.'
She could have smuggled out a dozen boxes of defunct
pigeons under its voluminous folds.

Her mother was unsuspicious as Bettina crossed
through the kitchen again, wearing the cape. She neatly
blocked Adolf's rush for the opening door with one foot
and slipped through.

The rain seemed to be lighter, although still relentless. The ground was mere tufts of grass drooping above a sea of mud and puddles. What daylight there had been was rapidly disappearing, making the world gloomier than ever.

She turned sideways to slip through the barely discernible gap in the hedge between the two houses, feeling the waterlogged branches drag against her, tipping torrents of water down her raincape, her legs and into her shoes.

She used a few words that would have shocked her mother and shook herself thoroughly as she gained the shelter of Zoe's little back porch with its overhanging roof.

The lock fought the key – she had mentioned this to Zoe before – then capitulated so abruptly that she was afraid the key had snapped. She turned the knob and the door swung open with a loud creaking protest suggesting that it was in terminal agony and this was its last cry before expiring.

The house seemed warm in those first few moments of shelter from the storm, then the chill began to make itself felt. Zoe and her mother had obviously turned off the central heating before they left. She removed her raincape and hung it on the hook by the door.

Her footsteps echoed on the linoleum as she crossed the kitchen to the larder. The freezer clicked on with a raucous whine as she lifted the lid, startling her. Her nerves weren't what they used to be, no doubt about that. And an illicit horde of diamonds wasn't going to help.

Three pairs of tights lay on top of one of the stacks of ready-prepared meals. She must remember to ask Zoe if freezing really did lengthen the life of tights. Perhaps a shoe box wouldn't look so out of place to anyone investigating the freezer who saw the tights first. Nevertheless, she burrowed down into the chest, ramming the shoe box into the centre of the stacks and rearranging the food packages so that they hid the box.

She must warn Zoe that the box had been added to the contents of her freezer; it would be most upsetting if Zoe

41

came across it unexpectedly and opened it, thinking it was some new meal her mother had cooked and frozen. And Mrs Rome might have a heart attack if she were to discover such an abomination while innocently browsing through the freezer for something to tempt her appetite.

Unlike her own, Zoe's freezer was full enough not to warrant any additional packing in the way of towels or newspapers, so she closed the lid and went back into the kitchen. Everything was just the way it should be. She decided on a quick tour of the house, just to make sure the storm hadn't found any chinks in the armour. It shouldn't have. Zoe and Mrs Rome, she recollected wistfully, had managed to replace their roof last year. It would still be strong and watertight.

Feeling guilty, she took her time strolling through the house and even gave way to the temptation to slump into Zoe's rocking chair in the living room and just sit quietly for a few minutes. She relished the peace and quiet so much she seriously considered inventing some slight problem over here which would need to be watched, so that she could slip over occasionally and get a bit of peace.

In fact, Zoe had suggested this just before she left: 'Tell her we're having trouble with the boiler and you have to keep popping over to make sure it isn't going to explode.'

'Oh, no, I can't say that. She'd never stop worrying about it. There'd be no peace at all.'

'Well, then, say Bluebell gets homesick and you have to bring her over for a couple of hours every night. You'll be all right in the daytime, you can stay out in the garden. It's those long nights cooped up alone with Old Worryguts you've got to watch. You're still too young to be driven mad.'

'Madness might be a relief.' She had only been half joking. 'I wouldn't notice so much then. I'd be in my own little world.'

'It might be worse.' Zoe frowned at her uneasily. 'You might slip away into *her* little world and you'd both be mad together.'

42

'She's not really mad,' Bettina had protested. 'No madder than *your* mother.'

'You think *that's* a recommendation?' They had both dissolved into helpless giggles.

They could say these things to each other as to no one else. Each was the sister the other had never known – and without the sibling rivalry shared parents engender.

Mrs Bilby and Mrs Rome had moved into their adjoining houses as brides and formed a firm friendship, strengthened when they both gave birth to daughters within days of each other. They had named the girls after top models rather than after film stars as was the fashion then. Later, they frequently pointed out to their growing daughters that models married into the aristocracy more often than film stars did.

Alas for fond mothers' dreams. Neither girl had shown the slightest inclination towards the catwalk – or the aristocracy. Nor had there been any more children; both mothers seemed to feel that they had done their duty by providing a playmate and companion for each other's child. The girls were in and out of each other's houses so often that in moments of exasperation each mother was wont to exclaim that she had two daughters, after all.

Perhaps it had been an ideal way to grow up, but one pays for everything eventually. The bill arrived suddenly in their late twenties when Mr Bilby and Mr Rome went off on a fishing trip – or possibly poaching salmon, given Mr Rome's predilections – and were both drowned. Bettina and Zoe suddenly found themselves the breadwinners and noticed that all pressure to marry into the aristocracy – or to marry at all – suddenly disappeared. Any suitors who appeared in the following years had been frightened away by one mother or the other. No young man with any sense wanted to be saddled with the Mother-in-law from Hell.

It was another bond they shared – one they could have done without.

*   *   *

Bettina sighed and rose to her feet. She could not prolong the pleasant interval any longer but, yes, Zoe had been right. She must invent some excuse—

A loud hammering on the common wall and her mother's voice was shouting anxiously. She couldn't distinguish the words, but their purport was clear enough: she had overstayed her time and her mother was worrying.

'All right, I'm coming,' Bettina shouted back and gave the wall a thump for good measure.

She sighed again deeply as she swirled the raincape around her and stepped out into the dwindling storm.

It was going to be a long weekend.

The night, too, was longer than she had expected.

Mrs Bilby had decided to go to bed early and insisted that her daughter should do the same.

'And don't bring any of those cats upstairs with you,' she grumbled. 'They're a nuisance as they are. I won't have them running all over the house.'

The cats all turned to glare at her, narrowed eyes and lashing tails making their feelings clear. All were accustomed to spending the night on a soft bed next to a warm human and they had been hoping that last night had been a mere aberration.

'I'll see to it.' Bettina deftly captured the cats and inserted them into their respective cases.

The hysterical curses of the affronted cats followed them all the way up the stairs and could be heard in the bedrooms above.

'Pay no attention,' Mrs Bilby said. 'They'll settle down when they see that their behaviour isn't getting them anywhere. And this is the last time you pull a trick like this, young lady. I'll never know what possessed you to take on so many cats!'

Bettina gave a sigh for the thought that no one except her mother had called her young lady for a long time now. Probably Mrs Bilby still thought of herself as middle-aged,

44

not noticing that her daughter had now attained that status herself.

'Good night, Mother.' Bettina went into her room and closed the door, resisting any temptation to defend herself. She certainly could not have explained the circumstances to her mother – Mrs Bilby would have enjoyed them too much.

It was quite unfair to blame Bettina for *all* the cats. Pasha had been an unintended last-minute addition to the crew.

A distraught Sylvia had waylaid her on her way home from work Thursday night, a Sylvia trembling and on the verge of tears.

'Oh, please help,' Sylvia had pleaded. 'I *have* to go to Edinburgh for the weekend with Graeme. If you could only take care of Pasha for me – he won't be any trouble.'

'I don't know . . .' Bettina had hesitated, thinking of the three cats she had already agreed to care for.

'I— I'll tell you the truth,' Sylvia had suddenly blurted out, pushing a shaking hand through her already dishevelled hair. 'Oh, God! It's so awful! I can't bear it. I don't know what to do. Yes, I do. I'll go up to Edinburgh and confront them!'

'Them?' Bettina was faintly horrified at the implication of that. Sylvia and Graeme, although they had only lived in the neighbourhood for a relatively short time, about two years, had always seemed an ideal couple and very happy together.

'He's got a woman up there! He doesn't think I know it. He goes up there all the time. Business trips, he says.' She gave a short ugly laugh. 'I know what kind of business now!'

'I'm so sorry. If there's anything I can do . . .' With a sinking heart, Bettina realized she had just fallen into the trap.

'Take care of Pasha for me.' Sylvia pounced. 'It's too late to get him into any cattery now – they're all booked up for the Bank Holiday weekend.'

'Yes, they would be.'

'I didn't know I was going to do this.' Sylvia fixed her with desperate eyes. 'But suddenly, I can't stand it any more. I've got to see what she looks like, how they look together—' She broke off with a choking sob.

'All right.' Bettina would have agreed to more than that to escape this embarrassing scene. 'All right, I'll look after Pasha.'

Bettina shuddered again at the memory and wondered how Sylvia was faring in Edinburgh. On that sombre thought, she turned off the light and, thoroughly exhausted by the problems of the day, fell asleep.

But not for long. This time it wasn't the cats who awakened her. The house was silent, but the feeling of having been suddenly and uneasily disturbed remained.

Had her mother called? She shuffled into her slippers and pulled on her robe, her disquiet growing. Was it too quiet? By now, her mother should have called again. Unless she couldn't . . .

She padded along the hallway to stand, one hand on the doorknob, listening outside her mother's room. Silence. Deep silence. Carefully, she turned the knob and inched the door open.

Still silence. As her eyes adjusted to the darkness, she saw the pale oblong of the windows across the room; the windows overlooking the street, outlined by the rim of light around the curtains.

Belatedly, she recognized that part of the silence could be attributed to the fact that the rain had stopped. So had the wind. Had anything . . . anyone . . . else?

She held her breath, listening, straining her eyes to catch any faint rise and fall of the bedcovers.

Then, in the distance, she heard it. The sound that had wakened her. The muffled roar of a powerful motor. Outside, coming closer. The rim of light around the windows brightened as headlights moved slowly down the street.

At this hour? After such a storm? Unless they were lost.

Or the storm had brought down more trees, blocking the major road, so that the traffic was being detoured along this normally quiet street.

She tiptoed across the room and twitched the curtains aside slightly, looking down on the street. Instantly, she had the unnerving feeling that she was being observed herself. She shrank back involuntarily, retaining enough presence of mind to hold the curtain still, so that no one looking up could tell whether it had been carelessly drawn or recently moved.

The sleek dark limousine rolled past at a stately pace, as though leading a funeral procession. But no other cars followed it. She leaned forward to watch its slow progress to the end of the street, where it turned and began to retrace its path. The growl of its engine rose to an ominous roar as it came closer; she would know that engine again when she heard it.

'Bettina!' The sudden cry made her jump. 'What are you doing there? What's the matter?'

'Nothing, Mother.' Bettina retreated from the window, fingertips to her lips to signal silence, as though their voices could be heard by anyone inside the passing car. 'It's all right. Go back to sleep.'

'Sleep? I haven't slept a wink all night. There's too much disturbance going on. I told you we'd have no peace with all those cats.'

'The cats haven't made a sound,' Bettina said firmly, hoping she was right. 'You've been asleep and dreaming.'

'I have *not!* And you haven't answered me. What are you doing in here?'

'Just looking out of the window. I thought I heard something outside . . .' The car had reached the end of the street and was turning again.

'No,' she said quickly, as her mother stretched out a hand towards the bedside lamp. 'Don't turn the light on.'

'Why not?' But the hand fell back to the mattress, almost with relief.

'It will wake you up. You want to go back to sleep.'

'I tell you . . . I won't . . .' Mrs Bilby's voice was fading, only the need to argue keeping her awake.

Outside the limousine cruised slowly past and reached the other end of the street. This time it turned away, but not very far away. Bettina heard it drive slowly down the parallel street.

Someone lost and looking for the right address . . . probably.

'Sleep . . .' she repeated softly, hypnotically (she hoped). 'Go back to sleep . . .'

With a soft huffling sigh, her mother relaxed and her breathing became slow and even.

Bettina tiptoed to the door, closing it softly from the outside, and stood for a moment in the hallway, still listening.

In the distance, the heavy motor droned monotonously.

From below, a faint questioning yowl sounded tentatively.

Adolf. Awake and wondering if anyone else was.

Still tiptoeing, she gained her room and closed her door firmly. She was going back to sleep herself.

CHAPTER 5

In the morning, a pale sun shone weakly on a waterlogged world. The television news yielded its fresh quota of highways under water, bridges washed away, trees blocking roads, houses without roofs, scaffolding collapsing, abandoned cars with nothing showing above water but the roofs, bodies of cattle and sheep floating down swollen rivers, ships in distress off the coast, major structural damage to buildings ashore, and all the other tragedies, disasters and calamities following in the wake of the storm.

Weather pundits speculated cheerily as to whether all this meant that meteorological patterns were changing and the country was due for a bitter winter, or whether the storm was simply a freak happening.

A panel of experts, chuckling merrily, were just agreeing that it might be an abnormally bad winter when Mrs Bilby hit her remote control and had the satisfaction of seeing the screen go dark.

'They don't have to be so bloody happy about it,' she grumbled. 'You can tell *their* roofs don't leak.'

'I'll get someone to see to it as soon as the holiday is over,' Bettina promised recklessly. Anything to head off another litany of complaints.

'And what do you think you're going to use for money?' her mother challenged. 'I've told you before, I'm not standing for a second mortgage on this house, no matter if it falls down around our ears. We've got all we can do with the one we've got – and it's only another eight years until we're free of it.'

Only! Another eight years! And that was if all went well. If she lost her job, or fell ill . . .

'We'll manage somehow,' she said. 'The work's got to be done or the place *will* fall down around our ears.' She was suddenly aware of a warm, almost hot, feeling emanating from the cylinder in her pocket.

Burning a hole in her pocket. Dare she use one of the diamonds? How could she go about converting it into cash? *No! No!* Resolutely, she pulled her mind away from the temptation.

'Well, I don't see how.' Her mother looked at her suspiciously. 'Unless you've got some savings I don't know about.'

'There's only the bit we're saving up for a holiday. We could—'

'Oh, no, we couldn't! That's my once-a-year chance to get away and have a bit of a rest. I'll see the hallway knee-deep in water before I give that up.'

'You may not have long to wait.' She could not keep the bitterness out of her voice. She discovered that her hand was clutching convulsively at the cylinder. Adolf watched her with hopeful interest; all sorts of goodies came from hands thrust into cardigan pockets.

'You'd better empty those buckets again, but don't put them away. The roof will be dripping for ages yet and it may start raining again. I don't trust this weather.'

It had been a long time since Mrs Bilby had trusted anything or anyone, but there was nothing to be gained by pointing that out.

'I'll see to the buckets right now,' Bettina said.

'If they're too full, dip a bit out with a saucepan.' Her mother followed her into the front hall. 'You don't want to strain yourself—' She broke off abruptly and moved forward to look out of the narrow window flanking the front door.

'Here! What are those men doing out there?'

'What men?' Bettina tried to look out, but her mother

50

blocked the view. She stepped into the living room and stood behind the curtains of the bay window.

She could see them clearly now: two men with long poles, poking about in what seemed to be a small pond stretching from the pavement to the middle of the street about three houses down. The pond had not been there Friday night.

'What are they doing?' Mrs Bilby demanded, joining her behind the sheltering curtains.

'Trying to unblock the drain, I'd say.'

'If you ask me, I'd say they can't even *find* the drain. Just look at them, fishing around with those poles. They're nowhere near it. Typical incompetence! And we pay our rates for this!'

The cats, taking advantage of the open door, clustered around their ankles, ready to join in whatever was going on, even an indignation meeting. It was probably a treat for them to see Mrs Bilby indignant about something besides themselves.

Bluebell eeled around the curtain and leaped up on the windowsill, followed immediately by Enza. Adolf remained on the other side of the curtain, but lurched up to rest his front paws on the windowsill and look out. Pasha hurled himself against Bettina's ankles with a mournful plaint; he was missing the attention he usually got from Sylvia.

Bettina gathered him up absently and stroked him as he settled down in her arms, staring complacently through the curtains from his now-superior viewpoint.

One of the men straightened up and looked around uneasily, as though sensing the combined gaze of all those watching eyes. He said something to his companion, who also straightened, rubbed the small of his back and peered around near-sightedly.

The first man said something else, took what appeared to be a mobile phone from his pocket and pulled out the aerial, holding the phone to his ear. The younger man took advantage of his superior's incoming call to rub his back again and do a few stretching exercises. He did not appear to be accustomed to manual labour.

The older man began to pace up and down the pavement, leaning over slightly to peer into the lagoon along the kerb as he walked. When he turned abruptly, he caught the younger man doing a knee-bend and snapped something at him.

Guiltily, the young man began wielding his pole again, moving to a fresh position beside the pool, while the other slammed down the aerial and replaced the phone in his pocket.

'That was a short telephone call,' Bettina said.

The older man swerved suddenly in her direction, almost as though he had heard her.

'Don't let them see us!' Mrs Bilby stepped back, obeying the cardinal Suburban Commandment: Thou shall not get caught spying on your neighbours.

Bettina moved back with her, but the cats remained in place, shamelessly staring at the unexpected entertainment outside.

The older man shook his head and stepped back – but not fast enough, as a sudden movement from his subordinate sent a tidal wave swooshing across the pavement. He looked down at his sodden shoes gloomily, shook his head again and started away towards an unmarked van parked near the corner of the street.

As he passed the house, the array of cats in the window obviously caught his eye. He stopped and stared at them. They stared inscrutably back. After a moment, he continued on his way.

'They don't even know how to dress for their job these days,' Mrs Bilby said. 'Fancy not even wearing boots. Did you see those shoes? Ruined! They were never intended to go splashing about in puddles.'

The rest of the man's wardrobe had not been designed for all-weather wear, either, Bettina noted. The dripping trouser ends were pinstriped and the raincoat was from one of the designers more noted for fashion than practicality.

The younger man was more suitably dressed in jeans and a duffle coat, but Bettina suspected that anyone who took a close look would discover an exclusive label on the jeans and the coat was obviously new and expensive.

Neither of the men looked happy about the position they found themselves in. It was obviously above and beyond the call of ordinary duties.

'The Water Board must be pretty desperate to send those two out on a job,' Mrs Bilby said. 'They haven't even got the right equipment with them.'

'After this storm, the situation probably *is* desperate,' Bettina said. 'They'll have sent out anyone they can muster as emergency crews. All hands to the pump—'

'And where *is* the pump? They probably started out as plumbers,' Mrs Bilby sneered. 'They'll have to go back and get their tools.'

'Perhaps they're from the council.' Bettina wasn't sure she believed that, either.

'And working on a Bank Holiday Sunday? Storm or not, that's a laugh!'

The man still working gave a shout, tugging at his pole which appeared to be stuck. The older man went running back. They both fought with the pole, trying to free it from whatever had caught it.

'They'd better be careful,' Mrs Bilby said darkly. 'Else they'll do themselves an injury. That's no way to—'

The pole bent almost double, then sprang straight again. The younger man staggered back, clutching his forehead.

'Utterly useless!' Mrs Bilby said happily. She edged forward and twitched the curtain aside, her natural caution forgotten in the desire not to miss any of the entertainment.

The older man retained his hold on the pole and said something short and probably sharp. The younger man squared his shoulders and advanced to renew his own grasp on the pole. They began rocking it to and fro, slowly at first, then more quickly. At what appeared to be a command, both men heaved upwards on it.

For a moment, nothing happened, then it yielded abruptly, sending them off balance. The older man lost his grip and lurched forward, landing on his hands and knees in the middle of the huge puddle.

'Tears before bedtime!' Mrs Bilby crowed triumphantly. 'What did I tell you?' She leaned forward avidly, so restored to good humour that she actually patted Adolf's head before thrusting him aside.

'And look at that – it's not even a pole. That's a garden rake they've got there, an ordinary garden rake. Talk about no equipment!'

'It seems to have done the trick,' Bettina said. 'The water's going down.'

A large clump of matted leaves was caught in the tines of the rake. The young man began pulling at them. The older man struggled to his feet, his lips moving. It was probably just as well they couldn't hear what he was saying. He brushed ineffectively at the water cascading off his clothing.

His cohort's shoulders hunched against the obviously uncomplimentary tirade, but he continued tearing away the leaves and hurling them from him.

'Look at that,' Mrs Bilby complained. 'He's throwing them all back where they'll block the sewer again. The man's an idiot! Why doesn't the other one stop him? *One* of them ought to know what they're doing.' She was so incensed she appeared on the verge of rapping on the windowpane and calling out to them.

'Don't!' Bettina caught her hand as she raised it.

'You're right.' Mrs Bilby backed away hastily. 'Attract their attention and they might want to come in here and dry off. Let them go back where they came from.'

The wetter one appeared to be arguing just that. The younger man nodded, but continued to rake frantically at the receding waters. He stirred up more leaves, occasional twigs and branches and miscellaneous waterlogged objects, all of which he scrutinized carefully before throwing them back into the water.

'What does he think he's doing?' Mrs Bilby demanded. 'He's sure to block up the sewer again if he doesn't stop.'

'But the water is still going down.' Bettina tried to look on the bright side. 'Maybe they *do* know what they're doing.'

'More luck than judgement, if you ask me,' Mrs Bilby sniffed.

Both men stopped what they were doing and turned to watch as a small battered blue van appeared at the end of the street and drove slowly past them.

'That's odd,' Mrs Bilby said. 'You don't often see this road so busy on a Sunday – especially with everyone away and after the storm we've had.'

'Perhaps the storm has done more damage locally than we know about.' Bettina felt a growing uneasiness. 'They seem to be looking for something, too.'

'They've certainly been driving around in mucky places. Just look at how filthy that van is – even the numberplate is so covered in mud you can't read it.'

That was the thing that had been bothering her. One of the things. She looked towards the sleek but anonymous van parked at the corner. The numberplate on that was also obscured by mud and leaves. Had both vehicles been driving through the same rough terrain? And why?

More to the point: why had they both wound up in this quiet suburban street?

Or had they? The moving vehicle had reached the end of the road; it turned and drove out of sight.

The two watching men turned back to their work in a slightly bemused manner. The small pond had disappeared into the sewer, leaving a thick residue of mud and leaves. They stared down at it and they did not appear to know what their next move should be.

They conferred briefly, the older man adding weight to his argument by plucking at his sodden trouser leg and shaking it at his confrère. For good measure, he sneezed.

The younger man nodded gloomily and they started back towards their van, keeping to the gutter and stopping to kick at lumpy objects along the way.

'There's something not right about those men,' Mrs Bilby said. 'Do you think we should call the police?'

'I thought you didn't trust the police.'

'Not with anything valuable, but they ought to be able to deal with criminals. Or lunatics.'

The sky had grown dark again. Large lazy drops of rain began plopping slowly against the windowpane.

The two men looked heavenwards and their lips moved. They did not appear to be praying.

There was the sound of a car motor immediately ahead of them and they snapped to attention, staring in the direction of the sound.

Bluebell leaped to her feet and began dancing up and down the windowsill, her plumed tail waving a welcome. Bettina did not have to look to see who it was.

'Zoe's back,' Mrs Bilby said unnecessarily. 'Do you suppose something's gone wrong?'

The neat little Fiesta sailed down the street and pulled to a halt in front of the house next door. It was the first vehicle Bettina had seen all day with readable numberplates.

Bluebell began purring loudly. The two men turned to survey the car and its occupants while still moving towards their own van.

Zoe got out, waved cheerily to Bluebell and stared with open curiosity at two drenched men walking backwards. Her mother struggled out on the passenger side and stood on the pavement, also looking at the two strangers behaving so oddly. She said something and Zoe laughed.

Obviously stung, the men swung around and marched purposefully to their waiting van and leaped into it, slamming the doors vehemently. The engine roared and the van took off.

Zoe looked after the van with mild surprise then turned to the window and shrugged, giving another little wave with the twirl of the fingers that signalled 'Be round later'. Her mother was already halfway up the path to their front door. Zoe removed two suitcases from the car, locked the door and followed her.

'They *look* all right,' Mrs Bilby said grudgingly, turning away from the window now that the show appeared to be over. Bluebell raced her to the door and began agitating to be let out; she wanted to go home, now that Zoe was back.

The other cats decided that they just wanted to go out. They gathered behind Bluebell and raised their voices.

'There they go again!' Mrs Bilby said. 'My nerves can't stand this. Let them out!'

'It's pouring,' Bettina protested automatically. 'I'll pop Bluebell home; that will be one less to worry about.' And it would give her a chance to warn Zoe about the unexpected addition to her freezer.

How much else should she tell her?

'You'd best empty those buckets before you do anything else.'

Damn the buckets! She barely stopped herself from saying it aloud. Her nerves were fraying worse than her mother's – and with better reason. If only the buckets were all she had to worry about.

'I'll do it now,' she said meekly and escaped into the hallway, conscious of Bluebell's accusing look.

Just about in time. Large dollops of water were plopping into the buckets. Another half-hour and they'd be brimming over. Had the holes in the roof grown larger? Or had a slate or two blown off in the storm? She'd have to cross the street and try to inspect the state of the roof with the old opera glasses that had belonged to her grandmother. Just as well the inept workmen had managed to unplug the sewer and drain away the floodwater; it would be too much if she'd have to go wading as well.

She positioned the empty buckets under the leaks, watching glumly as the water fell into them with a hollow splash. The leaks were definitely worsening. If this rain didn't stop soon . . .

'Bettina!' Her mother's voice rose in a shriek. 'Bettina! Come down here at once! Now those men are swarming all over our garden!'

'Burglars!' Mrs Bilby stood well back from the window and glared out at the workmen at the bottom of the garden. 'That's what they are – burglars! Sneaking around under cover of the storm to see who's away for the holiday weekend, so they can back up a lorry and carry off the contents of the whole house. I knew it!'

'They're not the same men,' Bettina said thoughtfully. These looked more like genuine workmen, properly dressed for the job with thigh-high waders and heavy oilskins. Like the others, they carried long poles and kept prodding the bushes with them. Like the others, they appeared to be unhappy and bad-tempered, communicating in short bursts, jaws thrust forward pugnaciously and eyes snapping.

'I don't think any of them can be burglars,' Bettina said. 'Burglars wouldn't make such a spectacle of themselves. Everyone in the neighbourhood who stayed home must be watching them.' The cats had already jumped up on the windowsill to stare out at the renewed entertainment appreciatively.

'A lot you know about it! What are they doing all over the place then? What are they looking for?'

'Isn't there a drain leading into the main sewer down there some place?' Bettina suggested carefully. 'Perhaps that's blocked too.'

As she and her mother watched, the men had another short altercation, then turned and stumbled around the hedge into Zoe's garden where they ignored the wide sweep of underwater lawn and began prodding at the hedge on that side.

'Telephone Zoe,' Mrs Bilby urged. 'Warn her about what's going on out there. Tell her to lock away her valuables.'

'Why don't we just call the police if you're that nervous?'

'Them!' Mrs Bilby had changed her mind again. 'A lot of use they'd be with burglars! You saw that newspaper. They'd probably just join forces with them for a cut of the loot.'

'I shouldn't think they could find enough valuables in this neighbourhood to make it worth their while.' As she spoke, Bettina felt a slight pang, her hand went guiltily to her pocket, the contents of which alone would be worth any amount of a burglar's time and attention. But no one could possibly know about that . . . could they?

'Sylvia Martin's house is full of fancy silverware and gewgaws. And those horrid modern paintings. She's always boasting about how much they're going to be worth, although I wouldn't give them houseroom myself.'

Pasha stirred restlessly and turned to give Mrs Bilby a hostile look, almost as though he could recognize criticism of his mistress – and resented it.

'They're emergency crews from the council or the Water Board – or both,' Bettina said firmly. Although . . . those unmarked vans cruising around had been big enough to accommodate any number of paintings. And the pin-striped gentleman and his expensively clad assistant looked as though they would be more at home strolling through an art gallery than splashing about in puddles.

'If you'd like,' Bettina offered, 'I'll go out and speak to them and ask for their identification.'

'And get your throat cut! You'll do no such thing!' Mrs Bilby went pale with horror.

'There goes Zoe . . .' Bettina's attention had been caught by a sudden movement. Zoe had opened her back door and advanced to the edge of her patio, holding her raincape over her head. As they watched, she called out and waved to the men.

'Mrs Rome must have sent her out to see what's going on.'

'That woman doesn't have the sense God gave to geese!' Mrs Bilby said. It was unclear which woman she meant.

Bluebell recognized Zoe and reared up, pawing at the windowpane and uttering excited cries. Adolf joined in, always willing to back up unreasonable demands.

'She'll come and get you later,' Bettina tried to calm Bluebell. 'She's busy right now.'

They watched as the two workmen at the bottom of Zoe's garden reluctantly decided that she *was* waving and gesturing to them and had another argument about it. Eventually the loser slowly waded up the shallow brook which had once been a path and joined Zoe at the edge of her patio, where she engaged him in spirited conversation. At least, it was spirited on her part; he looked rather dispirited himself. Until he raised his head and gave her a long malevolent look radiating hostility. Zoe, pointing towards the correct position of the drain, seemed oblivious.

'I'm going over there.' Bettina snatched up her raincape – the twin to Zoe's – and draped it over her head.

'Don't be stupid! You don't want to get involv—'

Bettina avoided her mother's clutching hand, blocked Bluebell's hopeful dash for the opening door with a foot, and ran out into the rain.

'Oh, Bettina . . .' Zoe turned, momentarily distracted, as Bettina came through the gap in the hedge. The workman took advantage of that to slip away. When she turned back, he was halfway down the path on his way to rejoin his workmate.

'What was that all about?' Bettina asked.

'Nothing good, I'm afraid.' Zoe frowned at the man's departing back. 'He isn't very articulate, but I gather we're in imminent danger of a flood if the situation doesn't improve.'

'A flood? Here?'

61

'Why not? Something seems to be terribly blocked up somewhere along the line. If they can't find the blockage and this rain doesn't stop, well . . .' Zoe shrugged. 'It looks as though we'd better start moving things upstairs. I'll help you roll up your carpets, then you can help me roll up ours.'

'If that isn't all I need!' Bettina's exasperation was mingled with relief. No wonder there were so many emergency crews swarming all over the place. It had nothing to do with—' Her hand crept to her pocket.

'At least, we ought to have plenty of warning,' Zoe said. 'With all these workmen around. Perhaps we could suborn one of them to help with the carpets.'

'I don't think my mother is going to want any of them coming into the house.' Bettina sighed heavily. 'She's got it into her head that they're burglars checking out the neighbourhood for likely houses to rob.'

'Oh, God!' Zoe shuddered. 'Don't let my mother hear that or we'll have two of them!'

'BETTINA! BETTINA!' They turned at the familiar call to see Mrs Bilby waving wildly from the front door. 'Come back here right now! Now there's a clipboard lady at the door!'

'I'd better go and see what that's all about.' Bettina started back.

'Maybe they're getting ready to evacuate,' Zoe said nervously. 'If the situation is as bad as those men think it is. Let me know.'

'If it's that bad, she'll be along to you next.'

'I wish we hadn't come back,' Zoe said unhappily. 'We should have stayed away – and we wouldn't have known anything about this until it was all over and there was nothing we could do.'

'Why *did* you come back?'

'Mother insisted. It was pouring in Bournemouth, too, and she said it was too depressing to bear. It reminded her too much of her honeymoon.'

*　　　*　　　*

62

The doorbell was chiming loudly and persistently. It had acquired an 'I-know-you're-in-there-and-you-might-as-well-answer-because-I'm-not-going-away' tone. The cats had lined up in the front hall and were watching the door with interest.

'All right, all right, I'm coming!' Mrs Bilby called, braver now that she had reinforcements behind her.

'Well?' she demanded, flinging back the door. Bettina caught Adolf just in time as he dived for the opening. The woman outside, not surprisingly, looked taken aback.

'I suppose you're from the council!' Mrs Bilby continued her attack.

The woman hesitated before answering. For a moment, she seemed to be contemplating the advantages of pleading guilty as charged.

'I hope you're sending round sandbags! We're going to need them soon.'

'Er, no.' The woman obviously realized there were no advantages in being from the council. 'I'm market research, actually.'

Bettina wondered if it would be possible to get a job in market research if Jelwyn Accessories folded; she hadn't seen anyone wearing clothes like that since the *Vogue* issue featuring the designer collections. The only problem was that she had never heard that market research paid that well – unless one happened to own the company.

'In this weather?' Mrs Bilby regarded her suspiciously. 'On a Bank Holiday weekend?'

'Overtime,' the woman said with a trace of desperation. 'We're paid extra for unsocial hours – lots extra.' She tried a confiding smile. 'And I can really use the money.'

Adolf sauntered forward and sniffed with great interest at the woman's Gucci shoes, as though detecting a strong odour of fish.

Bettina moved casually to the window and looked out. A jaunty, bright red foreign sports car was now parked at the end of the road.

'Er, do you think I might come in, please? I'd just like

to ask you a few little questions.' She brushed at a wet lock streaming out from under the Hermès scarf tied around her head, adding plaintively, 'And it's awfully wet out here.'

'I suppose so.' Mrs Bilby stood back ungraciously.

'Oh, thanks.' The woman rushed in before Mrs Bilby could change her mind. 'I'm most awfully grateful.'

Mrs Bilby sniffed and led the way into the living room. The cats regrouped and followed them.

Inside the door, the woman hesitated. She was not so young as she had appeared, Bettina was interested to see. 'Well preserved' was the description that sprang to mind. But the woman's attitude was still girlish. 'Oh, I don't want to drip all over your nice carpet . . .' She looked around helplessly. 'Perhaps I should take my coat off?'

'I'll hang it in the hall.' Bettina held out her hand for the Burberry raincoat, which was not as wet as it might be. 'Where's your umbrella?'

'Oh, I – I left it in the car.' The woman gave another ingratiating smile. 'It's so hard to juggle it along with a clipboard and handbag.' The long gilt chain of the bag clinked as she set the bag on the floor while she slipped out of her raincoat. The discreet suit underneath was also a Chanel worn over a turtleneck cashmere sweater. (How lucky the poor dear was able to earn a little badly needed overtime by working through the Bank Holiday weekend.) A heavy gold bracelet hung with chunky gold charms peeped from below one sleeve, the two charms on view depicted a TV screen – or possibly a computer screen, since a tiny mouse with an even tinier diamond for an eye, underlined the letter 'V' – and an artist's palette with sparkling coloured gemstones depicting the paint blobs and two brushes rising from the fingerhold.

It took all of Bettina's willpower to keep from putting her hand in her pocket and clutching protectively at her own little hoard of gems. She escaped thankfully to the front hall with the Burberry and took her time about arranging it on the hook on the old Victorian coat stand.

Another impulse came to her and this time she did not resist. She paused only a moment to listen and make sure that the woman was fully occupied in dealing with Mrs Bilby. Their voices drifted out to her reassuringly:

'Well,' the woman said, 'I guess I don't need to ask the first question. I can see the answer right here before me. You must be real cat lovers here.'

'I'm not,' Mrs Bilby denied fiercely. 'I hate the nasty little monsters!'

'Oh, er . . .' The woman sounded hopelessly confused. 'But you have so many . . . and such lovely ones.'

'Expensive, you mean. There's no accounting for the way some fools will throw their money around.' Bettina could tell from Mrs Bilby's tone that her mother was raking their visitor's outfit with a damning look; she didn't approve of wasting money on clothes, either, and even Mrs Bilby could recognize a Chanel suit.

'Oh . . . er . . . um . . .'

While the woman was floundering, Bettina took a deep breath and plunged her hand into one of the Burberry's pockets. It came out with a lace-trimmed handkerchief and a wedge of folded paper. Bettina gazed with wonder at the delicate scrap of sheer material surrounded by the deep lace border. Did people actually use something like that these days? They did – when they didn't have to worry about laundering it themselves.

She tried to unfold the paper noiselessly, pausing again to make sure there was no danger of being discovered by the others. They were still talking in the living room.

'Oh, dear,' Mrs Bilby was saying with grim relish. 'Did he ladder your nylons? Mind you, it wouldn't take much, they're very sheer. Ten denier, I suppose.'

'Seven, actually.' The voice seemed to be coming from between clenched teeth. 'It's quite all right. Oh!'

'Isn't that sweet?' Mrs Bilby gloated. 'He wants to get up on your lap. Pasha's taken quite a liking to you.'

'How nice.' There was a violent brushing sound.

'I'm afraid he's shedding a bit. We haven't had time to brush him today.'

'*Quite* all right.' The voice was cold enough to lower the temperature of the room. Mrs Bilby was not endearing herself to her visitor – nor did she intend to. '*Such* a beautiful cat.'

It sounded as though Pasha had their visitor well anchored. Bettina tilted the unfolded paper towards the dim light filtering in through the narrow side window. It was a map. A photocopy of a street map of the whole area, marked with a wide pencilled circle taking in an area of about a mile. Another dotted line circle marked a wider area outside the inner circle. The Bilby house was close to the centre of the inner circle. Several of the surrounding streets had neat little crosses marking—

'Bettina!' Her mother raised her voice. 'Bettina, where are you?'

Cursing silently, Bettina tried to refold the map along its original folds. Trust her mother to interrupt at a crucial moment! There was complete silence in the other room as they waited for her to answer. The map crackled loudly. Loud enough for them to hear?

Enza appeared in the doorway, looking curious. Her sharp ears had caught the sound. How long before someone else came to investigate?

There was a sudden clatter at the back door, an insistent knocking. Bluebell darted out of the living room and raced down the hallway.

'That must be Zoe,' Bettina called to her mother, using the sound of her voice to cover any further rustle as she shoved the folded paper back into the raincoat pocket. 'I'll get it.'

When she reached the kitchen, Bluebell was sitting beside the back door, casually washing a paw with an attitude of utter indifference.

'Who is it, then?' Bettina asked her, taking the precaution of looking out before opening the door. But it was

Zoe. Bluebell was obviously going to pay her out for going away and leaving her.

'It's raining harder than ever,' Zoe said, hurrying in. 'I suppose I'm glad we came back. Hello, darling . . .' She spotted Bluebell and stooped to scoop her up. 'Are you glad we came back?'

Bluebell abruptly dropped her aloof pose and gave Zoe a rapturous reception, then settled in her arms, purring loudly.

'Bettina! Bettina! Come in here and answer these questions. I can't understand them at all. Bring Zoe with you.'

'Questions?' Zoe arched an eyebrow.

Bettina shrugged and motioned Zoe to follow her.

'Sylvia! So you gave up on the weekend, too.' Zoe stopped and looked again. 'Oh, sorry. I thought you were Sylvia.'

'No.' The woman shook her head. 'No, I'm Viv. Vivien, actually. Vivien Smythe—' She stopped abruptly and one could almost see the hyphen hanging in the air.

'Sorry,' Zoe apologized again. 'But you *do* resemble her. And, of course, you've got Pasha.'

Pasha looked up at the sound of his name and muttered querulously. It was not Sylvia – that was his complaint, too. The soft material covering the lap was the same, the perfume was almost the same, but the fingers dabbing tentatively at his head were stiff and awkward and the face was different. He regarded Bluebell, purring smugly in Zoe's arms, with envy and discontent. She had her Zoe back again, but he did not have his Sylvia. Nevertheless, he had *someone*. He twisted his head to direct the clumsy fingers under one ear and gave an encouraging purr.

'Oh!' Vivien's face softened; her fingers relaxed into a caress. Pasha rewarded her with a louder purr. 'I think he really likes me.'

'And I thought you were here to work,' Mrs Bilby said.

'Right . . .' Shooting Mrs Bilby a venomous glance, Vivien picked up her clipboard and looked at the form clipped to it. 'I have your two names.' She nodded coldly to Mrs Bilby and Bettina. 'But not yours.' She looked at Zoe. 'Are you a member of the family, too?'

'Not quite,' Zoe said. 'I live next door.'

'Oh, good. Then I can do two houses at the same time.' She lifted the top page and began making notes on the second. 'You are . . . ?'

'Zoe Rome. Why do you want to know?'

So Zoe, too, thought there was something not quite right about Vivien Smythe.

'Oh, just a formality. You needn't worry. It's market research. If you wouldn't mind just answering a few questions.' Before Zoe could register any protest, she rushed on. 'Mrs Bilby has been explaining to me that she's just taking care of these cats over the weekend. Does that absolutely gorgeous cat belong to you?'

'Yes.' Zoe unbent a bit at the description. 'This is my Bluebell.'

'How sweet. Is she an only cat?'

'She is, at the moment. When she's a little older, I may breed from her.'

'Oh, fine.' Vivien ticked off one of the boxes on her form. 'That's very valuable to know. And what do you feed her? Dry cat food? Tinned cat food? Any special diet?'

'What sort of market research is this?' Bettina asked.

'It's for a pet food manufacturer,' Vivien said earnestly. 'They're exploring the possibility of expanding into new lines, checking up on how well the opposition is doing, making sure their product is satisfactory, thatsortofthing.' She ran the last words together nervously in her haste to finish the explanation.

'Which one?'

'Oh, well, I'm not sure I'm supposed to tell you that. But it's one of the big ones, one of the very big ones. Now . . .' She brandished her clipboard, grazing Pasha's back as she did so. He gave an indignant cry and jumped off her lap.

'Oh, I'm sorry, darling, I didn't mean to hurt you,'

Vivien apologized. Pasha gave her an injured look and withdrew to the far side of the room.

'It's all right,' Bettina said. 'He's just startled. He'll forgive you.'

'Good . . .' Vivien sounded happier. 'Anyway, with all these cats in the neighbourhood, I take it there aren't many dogs?'

'I had one,' Mrs Bilby said, 'but it died. There aren't any others around now. The cats have won.'

'Er, yes.' Vivien was momentarily disconcerted, then rallied. 'And I suppose . . . there aren't any birds, either?'

'Fat chance any bird would have with these little murderers around!' Mrs Bilby snorted.

'Would you like a cup of tea?' Bettina offered quickly, hoping to divert her mother before she blurted out anything else about birds. Especially dead pigeons.

'*What?*' She had succeeded. Her mother turned to glare at her. 'Have you gone mad, Bettina? We don't want tea now. It's nearly time for dinner.' Having made her point, she turned to Vivien and said with a carefully contrived show of hospitality, 'Of course, if you'd like a cup of tea, Miss Smythe . . . ?'

'No, no, thank you.' Vivien was thoroughly intimidated. 'I haven't time. There are so many more interviews I must get through. I really ought to be going.'

'If you're quite sure,' Mrs Bilby said with satisfaction.

'Quite.' Vivien cast a regretful look at the downpour outside. 'Quite sure.' She rose slowly to her feet.

'I ought to be going, too,' Zoe said. 'I'll have to ransack the freezer and get something out to start thawing for dinner.'

'Oh, no!' Bettina cried. 'I . . . I mean . . .' She was conscious of her mother and Vivien listening. She could not possibly explain anything to Zoe in front of them.

'I mean, I was just thinking. Why don't you and your mother come over here and we'll ring up for an Indian takeaway? They'll deliver and it's going to be a perfect night for a good curry feast. And it will save us doing any cooking.'

'What a good idea!' Zoe agreed enthusiastically.

'Well, I suppose we could do that.' Mrs Bilby was not going to betray any enthusiasm, but she dearly loved the occasional curry and it had been quite a long while since they'd had any. 'Are you sure they'll be open over the holiday? And do you think they'll be able to deliver in this weather?'

'You can depend on the Patels,' Bettina said. 'They're a large family, so the place is always open – and they'll deliver our order if they have to swim with it.'

Vivien had a wistful look as she slowly put on her Burberry and retied the Hermès scarf around her head. She gave the impression that she would much prefer staying in the pleasant little living room cuddling Pasha and sharing the curry feast to going out again into the chill downpour and resuming her canvassing of the neighbourhood.

Bettina closed the door behind her and stood watching.

As Vivien reached the gate, a man in a chauffeur's uniform and cap appeared suddenly. He, too, was carrying a clipboard and seemed to have come from the other side of the street. They conferred briefly, then moved off in the direction of the sports car.

CHAPTER 7

'Either she's the richest market researcher on record' – Bettina turned to Zoe, who was standing beside her, also watching – 'or she was lying about the whole thing.'

'Perhaps they're both market researchers, but the market research is really about something else,' Zoe said. 'Like class attitudes towards different types of researchers. So the questions themselves weren't important at all. That would make sense. She didn't seem to follow up on any of them and she gave up awfully quickly when your mother got a bit nasty.'

'Bettina!' her mother called from the living room. 'I believe I'd like that cup of tea, after all.'

'She would,' Zoe muttered. 'Mine is bad enough, but I don't know how you stand your mother sometimes.'

'Sometimes, neither do I,' Bettina murmured, then raised her voice: 'All right, Mother. I'll just go and put the kettle on.'

'I hope you throw it at her.' Zoe followed her into the kitchen, still urging the rebellion she would like to stage herself. 'She needn't have grudged that poor woman a measly cup of tea. Did you see how wet her shoes were? I hope she doesn't have to pay for them herself because she's ruined them.' Always erring on the charitable side, Zoe had evidently decided that her interpretation of the situation was the correct one.

'Mmm . . .' Bettina was not so sure. She filled the kettle while Zoe settled herself at the kitchen table, still cuddling Bluebell. The other cats drifted into the kitchen, drawn by the comforting sounds of food in preparation and hopes of getting some. Enza hopped up into a chair beside Zoe. Adolf and Pasha were placing their bets on Bettina and followed her from stove to fridge, alert and expectant.

'Uh-oh!' Zoe looked at the window in the back door where a dark shadow loomed against the glass. 'That's bad news if it's my mother – and it might be even worse if it isn't.'

The shadow looked too large to be Mrs Rome. Bettina opened the door a crack, leaving it on the chain, and was proved right. One of the workmen stood there, obviously waiting for the door to be opened enough to walk in.

'Yes?' She fended off Adolf with a practised foot, grateful that he was providing an excuse for not opening the door any wider.

'No, Adolf, you're not going out. You're not a Turkish Van – you can't swim.'

'Uh . . .' She had totally confused the man at the door. He regarded her uneasily, obviously losing track of what he was about to say.

'Yes?' She allowed an impatient note to creep into her voice. 'What *is* it?'

'Need to check yer cellar,' he muttered.

'We have no cellar.' It was not strictly true. They had a semi-finished room in the basement; her father had been working on converting the space into an extra room at the time he died.

'Yer loft, too. Need to check yer loft – an' yer roof.' The look he gave her dared her to tell him she had no roof.

'Don't let him in!' Mrs Bilby appeared in the kitchen behind her. 'Don't let anyone else in! I'm not having mud trailed through my nice clean house while they're snooping.'

'Sorry,' Bettina said. 'You can see how it is.'

'I could take my boots off,' he offered.

'Who is he? What does he want? Let me see his credentials – if he has any!' Mrs Bilby crowded in behind Bettina, a raging fury in defence of hearth and home.

'Never mind.' The man backed away nervously, keeping

a wary eye on Mrs Bilby. 'If yer gets flooded, it's yer own fault. Only tryin' to help.'

'And don't come back!' Mrs Bilby shrilled at his departing back. 'We know what you're up to! You're not fooling me! If I see you again, I'll call the police!'

'Poor man,' Zoe said softly. 'He's soaked through and chilled to the bone. He was probably just hoping for a cup of tea.'

'Well, maybe your mother will give him one.' Mrs Bilby sniffed triumphantly. 'He's over at your door now.'

'I'd better go.' Zoe thrust Bluebell into Bettina's arms. 'I'll collect her after the curry feast,' she promised. 'The house will have warmed up by then.'

'Don't let that man in,' Mrs Bilby warned. 'You'll find your house burgled next time you go away.'

The kettle was boiling and Bettina let Bluebell slide to the floor and turned away to make the tea. Her mother remained at the door, craning to watch what was happening next door.

'He's talking to them,' she reported. 'Zoe got over there just in time. Mrs Rome would have let him in, sure as fate.'

'Mmm-hmmm,' Bettina said absently. Adolf, Enza and Bluebell were gathered around her feet; Pasha slumped despondently against a table leg – losing someone who even resembled Sylvia had depressed him more than ever.

Had he had his cod-liver oil this morning? With everything else to think about, Bettina wasn't sure she had remembered. And, if he had, how much had he been able to keep for himself with all the other cats waiting to dive in and get it? Perhaps another spoonful of it might cheer him up. ('I often give him an extra dollop if he's been good,' Sylvia had said. 'He enjoys it so – and it's good for him.')

'Here, Pasha.' Bettina lifted him on to one of the kitchen chairs and poured a splash of cod-liver oil into a saucer. 'You have that all to yourself – and don't let the others take it away from you.'

Adolf immediately yowled a protest at this rank favouritism. He reared up on his hind legs and propped his forepaws on the edge of the chair, glaring at Pasha accusingly.

'No, Adolf.' Bettina struggled with Adolf, who suddenly seemed to have developed about six more legs, and finally got all four paws on the floor.

'She's shut the door in his face!' Mrs Bilby reported triumphantly from her observation post. 'But he's still standing there. She's never going to—'

'Perhaps Pasha won't mind if you have a little of his cod-liver oil.' Bettina used the bottle to lure the other cats away. 'Here, you can have some over here. Just leave poor Pasha in peace.' The cats converged on the saucer as she poured the golden liquid into it.

'She is! Well, I do despair! That Zoe is a prize fool! She's giving him two mugs of coffee.' Mrs Bilby shook her head at the stupidity she was witnessing. 'Treat them like that and she'll never get rid of them. They'll be expecting sandwiches next!'

'Zoe is very soft-hearted,' Bettina said. So was Zoe's mother. If Zoe had a mother like Mrs Bilby behind her, she would face the world with more suspicion and less charity. On the other hand, Zoe was going to have a lot better chance of getting help with rolling up her carpets if that became necessary.

'Just watch, she'll probably let them in when they come to return the mugs. She'll feel as though she knows them by that time.'

Bettina didn't comment. It was only too likely. And perhaps Zoe was right. It was not necessary to view the world as though it were peopled exclusively by enemies, potential enemies and criminals.

And yet . . . Bettina's hand went to her pocket again. Something decidedly odd and unsettling was going on. Apart from the storm, that is. The storm was complicating matters; it was not unnatural that emergency crews of all sorts should be out trying to control the damage being done by the flooding.

The storm was the cause of her problem. If it had been a fine night, the pigeon would have soared through the skies to its destination, arrived safely, and she would never have suspected that such strange things were happening elsewhere in the world.

Adolf backed away from the saucer, licking his chops, and looked at Bettina with eager interest. What else might she have in the way of delicious goodies tucked away?

Right now, the storm was her excuse for inaction. No one could blame her for not instantly reporting the treasure trove that had almost literally fallen into her lap. Not when there was so much to do and so many other things to worry about. (Was it time to empty the buckets again?)

Was it treasure trove? Perhaps not, since it hadn't been buried. Or did that necessarily apply? In any case, there ought to be some sort of reward given for the safe return of the diamonds.

Return to whom? How could she find out who owned one anonymous pigeon? And why was the pigeon so anonymous? She seemed to recall reading that tame pigeons were ringed with identification bands at birth – if only to separate them from the millions of other pigeons who flew around, heirs to all the natural hazards that creatures known to their enemies as 'flying vermin' were apt to encounter. Sudden death was endemic to the species, whether from small boys with air rifles, determined poisoners, traffic, or even cats.

Bettina thoughtfully returned Adolf's gaze. He was looking too innocent to be true, which probably meant he was plotting something. She'd have to keep an eye on him.

It was too bad she didn't know as much about pigeons as she knew about cats. Bettina tried to remember just what she *did* know about pigeons. Someone had once trapped her in a corner at a party and given her a long and tedious lecture on the subject. Who had it been? Random bits of it came drifting back to her.

Pigeons had always been used to carry messages, especially in wartime, from prehistory through to World War I when the legendary bird Cher Ami had even been decorated for his services. In the nineteenth century, a banking house had used them to gain knowledge of currency movements on the Continent well ahead of its competitors. Reuters news agency had found them invaluable. They had been used to carry word from cities under siege and from racetracks and sporting events. They had been invaluable in their time.

Improved telecommunications had gradually made them obsolete. And these days fax machines transmitted information instantaneously. But pigeons still had their fanciers, they were still pets. And they were still used, it seemed, for transmitting . . .

'Telephone, Bettina,' her mother said. 'Are you deaf? Answer the telephone.'

It had already tweetled several times, Bettina realized as she went into the hall and picked it up. The cats were there and regarding it with the exasperated, slightly frustrated expressions of those who suspected some sort of bird was enclosed in it and mocking them.

'Bettina, it's William.'

'Oh, William, yes. How are you?'

'How are *you* is more to the point. The news reports say we have flooding in low-lying areas. Is your house all right? Is Zoe's?'

That was the nub of the call. Zoe. Or . . . was it? William Simson, chief designer at Jelwyn Accessories, was friend and Old Faithful to (once he had met Zoe) both of them.

'It's pretty wet here, William,' Bettina said, 'but we're still above water. The whole street.'

'You're sure?' He sounded disappointed. 'I could come round and help. Do anything that's needful. I know you have your hands full looking after Zoe's place as well as your own.'

'Where are you then?' Bettina asked. 'I thought you were going to France for the weekend.'

'Not in this weather,' William said. 'The ferries were suspended. If I'd wanted to hang around for a couple of days until the weather eased, I might have got a sailing, but it didn't look likely the way the gale was blowing. Force nine, at least. The ferries weren't going out in that. So I gave it up as a bad job, turned around and came home.'

'So did Zoe.' Bettina decided to be magnanimous. 'It was storming in Bournemouth, too, so she and her mother have come back home. She's coping with things now.'

'Only coping?' William sounded cheered. 'And you? Perhaps I'd best come round and see what I can do to help.'

'If you like.' Bettina surrendered. It would be rather pleasant to have William to bear some of the strain. 'Zoe and her mother are coming over and we're ordering a curry feast, delivered. Come and join us.'

'. . . Good.' The pause had been only momentary, undoubtedly engendered by the thought of an evening with both Mrs Rome and Mrs Bilby. It was a standing, rather black, joke between Bettina and Zoe that the first one to lose her mother would be proposed to by William. At the same time, Zoe predicted, the odds were that some orphaned waif would rush in and nab William at the last minute. Such was life.

Not that William was the answer to a maiden's prayer, but he was eligible, solvent and moderately attractive . . . well, presentable. And women of a Certain Age didn't have that much choice available to them.

As it was, both mothers were hale and hearty and looked good for another decade or two, by which time the whole problem would be academic – always provided the threatened waif hadn't captured our William in the meantime.

'Bettina – you're a million miles away,' William accused.

'Oh, sorry.'

'I said: Can I bring anything along? Besides the bottle, that is. Anything at all you need?'

'Perhaps a few sandbags,' Bettina said. 'No, sorry,

William, only joking. I don't think we need anything. I did lots of shopping before the long weekend closed in. I didn't reckon on the storm but, as it's worked out, we have plenty of supplies to see us through.'

'Good. Well done. And Zoe? If she thought she was going to be away for the weekend . . .'

'Her freezer seems to be full,' Bettina said. 'I don't think she's going to need anything, either.'

'Good.' He did not sound entirely pleased. It must be awkward to be encased in armour, mounted, lance at the ready – and then discover that no maiden needs rescuing.

'Good. I'll be round in about an hour or so then.'

'Wear your wellies,' Bettina warned. 'And we'll look forward to seeing you.'

'Did I hear you inviting someone to dinner?' her mother asked pettishly as she returned to the kitchen.

'Only William. He changed his mind about going to France.'

'Not many people are getting anywhere this weekend,' Mrs Bilby said with relish. 'They should all have known better and stayed home.'

Bettina clenched her hands in her pockets and took a deep breath. 'You may be right,' she said in a neutral tone.

Adolf hurled himself against her ankles, purring loudly. Enza and Bluebell moved closer, as though to demonstrate solidarity – with her, not Adolf. Only Pasha continued to droop miserably, slumping against his carrying case in a defeated pose.

Bettina looked at him uneasily. She knew that cats condemned to six months' quarantine away from their owners did not survive as well as hardier – or more egotistic – species, like dogs. But surely Pasha couldn't sicken and die in a mere four or five days away from Sylvia.

Only . . . there was already something faintly wrong with Pasha. His failure to impregnate the Persian queens whose owners had paid such high stud fees was symptomatic of that. Was it the beginning of something more seriously wrong? He looked all right, he seemed all right

– apart from an increasing grumpiness. But he was accustomed to being an only cat and was unhappy with the competition he faced here. Was that all it was? Or was there something deadly eating away beneath the surface?

Really, Sylvia should have boarded him with the vet this weekend! Then he would have been under professional observation and a proper diagnosis of his condition might have resulted. Although the vet had checked Pasha over at the onset of his problem and pronounced him 'Basically fit, just a bit off-colour at the moment', Sylvia still suspected that Pasha was incubating some obscure disease. It was irresponsible of her to foist the responsibility for such a valuable cat on to someone else right now – even if she was fighting to save her marriage.

'Here, Pasha.' Bettina stooped and touched her finger to his nose anxiously.

'He's not sick, is he?' Mrs Bilby asked immediately. 'If he is, out he goes! I'm not having him throwing up all over the house. Shedding his fur everywhere is bad enough.'

'He's all right,' Bettina said. Pasha's nose was cold and wet. He twisted his head to slide her finger behind an ear that wanted scratching. Bettina obliged and he purred, looking at her hopefully; he also wanted a lap to sit in and a thorough cuddling.

Adolf blasted off an accusation of favouritism, snobbism and general unfairness. If there was a friendly lap going, *he* was entitled to it. Enza and Bluebell joined in the cry, complaining of neglect and abandonment. Bluebell especially was outraged; she knew Zoe was next door and *she* wasn't.

'I can't stand all this noise!' Mrs Bilby lurched to her feet, dashing the hopes of Enza, who had noticed there was a spare lap that might be available and had been edging closer. 'All this racket is giving me a headache. Make them be quiet.'

'All right.' There was only one sure way to do that. Bettina reached for the food and their dishes. The yowls

79

instantly changed to something softer and more appealing as they swarmed around her feet.

'Cupboard love!' Mrs Bilby sniffed. 'Greedy little monsters!'

'It keeps them quiet,' Bettina pointed out. 'That was what you wanted.'

'I don't want them at all! How you let yourself get talked into—'

'You were the one who agreed to take Enza.' And thank heaven for that. 'And we couldn't refuse Bluebell, we always take care of her when the Romes are away.'

'Bluebell and Enza are quiet little ladies, usually,' Mrs Bilby defended herself. 'It's those other two. A noisy spoiled little tyrant and a sick cat. Suppose he gets worse over the weekend? Suppose he dies? What would you do then?'

'We can always call the vet if Pasha seems worse.'

'We can't afford expensive vet's bills.' Mrs Bilby betrayed her real fears. 'I wouldn't like to rate our chances of getting any money back from Sylvia once we'd paid it out. If you ask me, she and that fancy husband of hers are mortgaged to the hilt – and beginning to know it.'

'Pasha will be all right,' Bettina said with an assurance she did not really feel. 'The weekend is half over. Sylvia and Graeme will be back Monday night. I'm sure Pasha can last out another forty-eight hours or so.'

Hearing his name, Pasha ambled over and rubbed his head against Bettina's ankles.

'Poor Pasha.' She gathered him up into her arms. 'You're not very happy, are you? Never mind, she'll be back soon.'

'What makes you so sure?' Mrs Bilby's voice had that taunting I-know-something-you-don't-know note in it.

'What do you mean?'

'You're not around during the day all week. You haven't seen what I've seen.' Mrs Bilby compressed her lips and nodded several times, radiating secret knowledge.

'What have you seen?'

'Well, I just happened to *notice*.' Mrs Bilby shrank back from the curtain-twitching implication of *seen*. 'In fact, it's been quite noticeable. Every time Sylvia Martin has left her house for the past two weeks, she's had a suitcase with her. Oh, she brings it back again in the evening, but it seems much lighter then. In the mornings, she's sometimes had trouble lifting it into the car.'

'So you think she takes out a full suitcase in the morning and returns with an empty suitcase in the evening?'

'I think they're moving out!' Mrs Bilby leaned back triumphantly and eyed her daughter to see how she was taking the news. 'Getting ready for a moonlight flit! I've seen it before, I know the signs.'

'There may be another explanation.'

'Name one!'

'Perhaps she was taking a lot of things to the dry-cleaners.'

Mrs Bilby's snort sent the cats scurrying for cover. 'The pawnshop, more likely!'

'Oh, really!' Her mother had taken a dislike to the Martins almost from the moment they had first moved in, but this was carrying it too far.

'Yes, really! Them with their fancy ways and forever insinuating how they've come down in the world because they've had to move into this neighbourhood.' She snorted again. 'If you ask me, they've got a lot farther down to go – and they're on their way again. And they're not taking any useless baggage with them – like a sick cat. You're going to be stuck with it.'

'Sylvia wouldn't abandon Pasha.' Bettina tightened her arms protectively around Pasha and he gave a soft protesting cry.

'Why not? She had great hopes for him – and he failed her. There he sits, the great lout, eating his head off and, when the time came, he couldn't pay his own way. He's just another expense – a loss. Why shouldn't she cut her losses and run?'

CHAPTER 8

There was a lengthening silence, while Bettina debated with herself as to whether to admit the real reason for Sylvia's impulsive flight to Edinburgh.

On the other hand, she had rarely known her mother to be wrong where the movements of the neighbours were concerned, although Mrs Bilby's interpretations were often faulty. The byplay with the suitcases had undoubtedly occurred; there must be a more reasonable explanation for it.

A sudden tap at the back door startled them both. Bluebell emerged from under the table and trotted to the door, looking up at it eagerly.

'That will be Zoe.' Bettina crossed to the door, which was already moving. Bluebell hurled herself at the opening.

'Mother will be along in a few minutes,' Zoe said, scooping Bluebell into her arms. 'If we order before she gets here, she wants a chicken curry and plenty of rice.'

'William's coming,' Mrs Bilby informed her.

'I thought he went to France.' Zoe was surprised.

'The weather disrupted the ferries, so he gave it up as a bad job and came back home,' Bettina said. 'He rang up to see how we were getting along.'

'Nice of him,' Zoe said absently. 'But he is nice. I really think you ought to marry him.'

'Funny, I keep thinking *you* ought to marry him.'

'Girls, girls, don't fight over him,' Mrs Bilby smirked, knowing she was perfectly safe. Bettina wasn't going to leave her for the likes of William.

'But you could do worse,' she added. 'Both of you.'

'We might wait till we're asked.' Zoe met Bettina's eyes and they exchanged guilty grins at what ending that wait entailed. If Mrs Bilby realized that William's choice depended upon the absence of a mother-in-law, she might lose what tolerance she had for him.

'A really clever woman could get herself asked.' Mrs Bilby preened herself in the knowledge that she was the only woman in the room who had managed to catch a husband.

'Hello, Pasha.' Zoe changed the subject, reached out to scratch one of Pasha's ears. 'How are you feeling today?'

'There's something wrong with that cat, if you ask me. Apart from the problem he's had for a long time, I mean.'

'Oh?' Zoe raised an eyebrow at Bettina.

'He's just missing Sylvia,' Bettina said. 'And the other cats are being rather beastly to him. They keep stealing his cod-liver oil.'

'Poor Pasha,' Zoe sympathized. 'She'll be back soon.'

'Hah!' Mrs Bilby said.

'Pardon?'

'Mother has her own ideas about that,' Bettina said resignedly.

'You're too trusting. You're just like your father. You'll believe anything anyone tells you.'

'Oh, no,' Zoe said under her breath. 'Don't tell me it's going to be one of those evenings.'

'There's William,' Bettina said with relief as the doorbell rang. 'He should help take the strain.'

'And there's Mum.' Zoe moved towards the back door. 'If we can get a good game of bridge or Scrabble going, there may be hope yet.'

It was amazing how easy it was to forget that one carried a fortune in diamonds in one's pocket. At first, the knowledge was ever present, then it came and went. The old adage *familiarity breeds contempt* was not strictly true — who could be contemptuous of those diamonds? — but familiarity eventually bred a certain amount of relaxation. Especially when coupled with the comforting realization that there was absolutely nothing one could do over a Bank Holiday weekend when most of Britain closed down. Add in the storm and the ensuing conditions and another day or two could be written off.

The curry feast around the kitchen table had been a great success. Filled with delicious food and surrounded by friends, a mellow mood had descended over everyone.

'Shall we have a game of cards?' Mrs Rome suggested.

'There are too many for bridge.' Mrs Bilby looked around with the beginnings of discontentment. She loved a good cutthroat bridge game. 'Someone would have to be left out.'

'I don't mind,' Bettina said quickly. 'I'll stay out here and do the dishes.' Domestic chores were preferable to partnering her mother at bridge.

'Why don't we settle for Scrabble?' Zoe pushed back her chair. 'Then it doesn't matter how many we have.'

'You go ahead.' Bettina waved them into the living room, beginning to clear the table. 'I'll still do the dishes first. No, I don't need any help.' She forestalled possible offers and turned back to the table to snatch the last remaining plate away from Adolf, who was doing quite a creditable job of washing it himself.

'If that curry gives you a tummy ache, you have only yourself to blame,' she told him.

Adolf hiccoughed and leered at her pleasantly. It would take more than a rich, spicy curry sauce to upset his digestion – and there would always be someone else to blame. For anything. He followed her over to the sink, licking his chops, his eyes alert for more opportunities.

Enza and Pasha were on the draining board, attending to the other plates she had put there. Adolf leaped up to join them, quickly saw that there was nothing left on the plates for him, and then had his attention caught by something outside. He moved forward to the window and stood looking through it intently, staring at something in the back garden.

'What is it, Adolf?' Bettina leaned over the draining board and the cats. 'Are those workmen out there again?' No, they couldn't be. It was pitch dark outside and they would have finished their shift and gone home ages ago. The rain had stopped and a pale and watery moon was trying to break through the remaining clouds.

'There's no one out there.' Bettina was trying to convince herself as much as Adolf. She laid a hand on his head and he gave a soft warning growl, still staring intently at something only he could see.

'That's enough of that.' She pulled down the shade, as though it might give some protection from whatever prowled outside. The kitchen immediately seemed warmer, cosier. It might give a false sense of security but, if they could not see out any more, it also meant that anyone outside could not see in.

The hum of conversation in the next room, acrimonious though it was becoming, brought a further sense of normality and security. It would be a foolhardy burglar who broke into a house teeming with people and cats.

Burglar, indeed! Bettina caught herself up sharply. That was her mother's fantasy, untarnished by the fact that there was nothing worth stealing in this house. Even Great-aunt Edwina's late-Edwardian silver tea service was so mass-produced and ugly it could hardly be worth much more than its melt-down value. Surely no self-respecting burglar would bother with that.

Diamonds, however, were another story. The realization swept over her again. She'd managed to forget them during the past few hours when they'd been occupied with ordering the food and listening to the complaints of Mrs Rome about the deficiencies of Bournemouth. Then William had launched into his sad story of the holiday lost in nose-to-tail traffic jams, cancelled ferries and motorway service areas where the food had run out, the tea was lukewarm and, though he was too genteel to do more than hint at it, the overworked toilets had given up the unequal struggle long before he reached them.

Mrs Bilby had blossomed like the flowers in May as she listened to these tales of woe. Other people's misfortunes always revived her, giving her the opportunity to emphasize her own wisdom in never leaving the house over a Bank Holiday weekend. One couldn't get into trouble that way.

Except when trouble came battering at the door; trouble could find one anywhere. Just staying at home, minding your own business, trying to be helpful to the neighbours by taking care of their cats – and look where it got you. Without the cats, she would never have known about the pigeon that had expired on the back doorstep. There would have been no reason to go outside and the gale-force winds would have eventually swept the pigeon somewhere else. Perhaps even down one of the open drains that hadn't yet been clogged by leaves and branches.

Diamonds down the drain. Her hand clutched convulsively at the cylinder in her pocket.

Adolf turned away from the now-viewless window and watched her with hopeful interest. Enza and Pasha abandoned the gleaming plates and dropped to the floor, strolling over to check their own dishes to see if they had been refilled yet.

'That is not a word!' Mrs Bilby's voice rose indignantly in the other room.

'It is in Urdu,' William defended weakly.

'*We* are English!' Mrs Bilby pointed out.

'The curry's gone to his head,' Mrs Rome jeered.

Poor William. It was a wonder he was willing to associate with them at all, when she and Zoe came with such drawbacks. Perhaps he liked to visit occasionally to remind himself of what life might be like if he were to weaken enough to declare himself to either of them.

The doorbell rang suddenly, followed by a startled silence in the living room.

'I'll get it,' Bettina called, glancing at her watch as she started for the front door. Nine forty-five. Who could be calling at this hour?

'Who is it now, Bettina?' her mother shouted before she had time to open the door. 'This place is busier than Waterloo Station at rush hour today.'

'Just a minute!' Bettina called, as much to the impatient visitor, who was now leaning on the doorbell, as to her mother. She paused beside the narrow window to peek out. The dark figure was male and vaguely familiar.

'Yes?' She opened the door, leaving the guard chain in place.

'Bettina, I'm sorry to disturb you at this hour.' The man stepped forward so that the light from the hallway illuminated his face. 'Is Sylvia here?'

'Graeme!' She stepped back, fumbling to release the chain. 'What are you doing here? I thought you were in Edinburgh.'

'Edinburgh? What gave you that idea? I've been in Brussels.' He stepped into the hallway. 'I just got back and I saw your lights on, so I thought I'd drop by and collect Sylvia and Pasha.'

'You can have Pasha,' Bettina said cautiously, trying to make sense of what she had just heard. 'But I'm afraid Sylvia isn't here.'

'Not here?' Graeme gazed at her in disbelief. 'Then where is she?'

'I thought she went to Edinburgh – with you.'

'I haven't been to Edinburgh.' Graeme spoke very slowly and clearly, biting off each word. 'I just told you. I've been in Brussels.'

'Who is it, Bettina?' her mother called again. 'Bring him in here.'

'Graeme . . .' Bettina caught his arm as he moved forward. 'Graeme, were you out in the back garden just a few minutes ago?' It was a silly question, she knew that as soon as she asked it. Graeme's shoes were moderately dry and polished, his trouser ends were definitely dry. If he had been in the back garden, he would have been soaked almost to the knees.

'Back garden?' Graeme stared at her incredulously. '*Whose* back garden? Why should I be in any back garden?'

'Bettina!'

'Oh, never mind.' She released his arm. 'Er, please don't pay any attention to whatever Mother says. She's . . . a little confused tonight.'

'Really?' The flick of Graeme's eyebrow told her that Mrs Bilby wasn't the only confused female around here tonight. Bettina followed him into the living room, feeling helpless in the grip of circumstances.

'So you're back, too,' Mrs Bilby greeted him. 'What's the matter? Road to Edinburgh washed away?'

'Why does everyone think I went to Edinburgh?' Graeme was beginning to look harassed.

Pasha came pattering out of the kitchen at the sound of the familiar voice. He gave Graeme a dismissive glance and looked around for Sylvia. She was not in sight. He circled Graeme, sniffing questingly at his shoes and trouser ends, then retreated under the card table where he sat down and brooded. It was all very unsatisfactory.

'But' – that was obviously Graeme's opinion, too – 'where *is* Sylvia?'

'I don't know,' Bettina said. 'She brought Pasha over on Friday afternoon and told me she was off to join you in Edinburgh.' Should she tell him what else Sylvia had told her? No, not with her mother and Mrs Rome listening so avidly. Besides, there was obviously something wrong with the story Sylvia had told her. It would be better to keep silent. Sylvia might come back at any moment with a perfectly reasonable explanation of her conduct; she was also quite capable of denying that she had ever said any such thing.

'She couldn't have said that.' Graeme was doing his own denying. 'She knew perfectly well I was in Brussels. I haven't been to Edinburgh in months. She couldn't have gone there. She knew I was coming home this weekend.

I'd have been here yesterday, if it hadn't been for the storm. The plane was diverted to Manchester and I had to take trains from there.' He looked around again. 'Where is she?'

'How do we know?' Mrs Bilby leaped into the fray. 'She came over here and dumped that wretched cat on us with scarcely so much as a by-your-leave and took off.' She added maliciously, 'She could be anywhere by now.'

Her mother didn't know how true that was. If Sylvia had deliberately told such an elaborate lie about her destination, then where was she? If she had really been removing her belongings from the house for the past fortnight, did that mean she was leaving Graeme?

If so, who was going to break the news to Graeme? Obviously, Sylvia had not left a note. Unless it was in the post. Tomorrow was Bank Holiday Monday, there would be no post delivered until Tuesday. And, if Sylvia had put a second-class stamp on it . . .

'She may have gone to visit her aunt in Erith.' Graeme had been giving the matter some thought. 'The old lady's been ill, perhaps she took a turn for the worse and rang Sylvia to come to her.'

'Much good Sylvia would be in a sickroom,' Mrs Rome muttered under her breath to Mrs Bilby.

'Yes, that must be it. She's gone to Erith,' Graeme decided to his own satisfaction, conveniently overlooking the world of difference between Erith and Edinburgh.

'You misheard, Bettina. Sylvia has gone to Erith and she wants *me* to join *her* there.'

'Perhaps so, but I'd telephone first, if I were you,' Mrs Bilby warned. 'You don't want to go paddling all over the country in these floods.'

'Thank you, I was intending to,' Graeme said coldly.

'She might not be there,' Mrs Rome pointed out.

William winced and Zoe said, 'Shush, Mum.'

'Well, thank you.' Graeme ignored the women at the table and spoke to Bettina: 'I'd better get along now. Sylvia may be trying to ring me. I'm sorry to have disturbed you.'

There was a brief commotion under the table and Pasha shot forward, skittering to a stop with his rump twitching indignantly. He glared back over his shoulder at Mrs Bilby's feet.

'Aren't you going to take your cat with you?' she demanded.

'He's not my cat.' Graeme and Pasha stared at each other with equal lack of enthusiasm. 'He's Sylvia's cat – and she isn't here just now.'

'Sylvia dotes on that cat,' Mrs Bilby goaded skilfully. 'She always said he was worth his weight in diamonds.'

'That was before we discovered he was firing blanks,' Graeme said bitterly.

'Really, Graeme!' Mrs Bilby drew herself up. 'There's no need to be coarse!'

'Sorry,' he said unrepentantly. 'You wouldn't really mind' – he appealed to Bettina – 'just looking after him for another day or so, while I get things sorted out?'

'Well . . .' Bettina hesitated. If Sylvia really *had* left Graeme, she had visions of Pasha becoming a permanent boarder – over her mother's dead body. Rather, more unfortunately, it would be over her mother's live and end-lessly nagging body.

'He's settled down nicely here,' Graeme said. 'And I can't possibly cope with him if I have to go to Erith and pick up Sylvia.'

'Oh, I suppose another couple of days won't make much difference.' Bettina hadn't spoken quite softly enough. She heard her mother's sniff and Mrs Rome's sotto voce rumble of sympathy.

'That's settled then.' Graeme made briskly for the door, ignoring the rumble of discontent behind him, although an uneasy flicker of his eyelids betrayed that he had heard it. Bettina began to suspect that Sylvia might have some-thing to be said on her side if she *had* departed.

'I *do* appreciate this.' Graeme paused before opening the front door and reached for his notecase. 'You'll need more cat food, I know. That thing eats like a horse. Nothing wrong with his stomach.'

'Well . . .' Bettina hesitated as he thrust the money at her, but knew her mother was listening in the next room. If she refused, she would never hear the end of it. 'He *is* running low on cod-liver oil.' No need to explain that was because he was perforce sharing it with the other cats.

'I'll bet he is!' Graeme's bitterness spilled over. 'The little bastard all but bathes in the stuff. His cod-liver oil bill would have kept Winston Churchill in cigars for a year!' He slammed the door behind him.

'How much?' Mrs Bilby asked avidly as Bettina returned to the living room.

'Twenty . . . No . . .' Bettina glanced down at the bank-notes in her hand. 'Thirty pounds.'

'That's a lot of cat food!' Mrs Rome exclaimed.

'It certainly is.' William pursed his lips with concern. 'Just how long does he expect you to keep the cat?'

'Who knows?' The same thought had crossed Bettina's mind – and William didn't know all the circumstances.

'We could—' Mrs Rome's eyes gleamed as she looked around the table. 'We could ask the cards.'

CHAPTER 9

'I hate it when she does this.' Zoe had followed Bettina
into the kitchen. 'She knows she hasn't got the Sight. The
Romany blood was all on my father's side – and a long
way back, at that.'

'A gypsy by osmosis?' Bettina suggested.

It wasn't much of a joke and Zoe awarded it a very faint
smile. 'You can laugh,' she said. 'It isn't your mother.'

'Mine is just as bad, in her own way.'

They both sighed. Bettina filled the kettle and set it on
the stove. The cats moved forward hopefully and formed
a guard of honour to escort her to the refrigerator.

'There!' The sudden cry from the living room startled
them all. 'There! What did I tell you?'

'You don't have to tell *me*,' Zoe muttered. 'She's turned
up the ace of spades – again.'

'Bettina!' her mother called. 'Bettina, come and look at
this!'

'I suppose we'd better humour them.' Bettina led the
way.

'Just look!' Mrs Rome said portentously. 'It's the ace of
spades! That means death!'

'Whose?' William looked around nervously. 'One of
us?'

'I thought you were going to find out how long Pasha
would be staying with us,' Bettina reminded her, a bit
brusquely. William was giving every indication of taking
the whole thing seriously. Another invisible black mark
against him.

'I told you that cat was sick!' Mrs Bilby declared. 'We've

got to get him out of here before he dies on our hands.'

'Pasha is perfectly healthy, apart from being sterile,' Bettina said firmly. 'He is *not* going to die.' She hoped she was right.

'Then who is?' Mrs Rome asked, as though she had produced incontrovertible evidence of an imminent demise. She stared ghoulishly at each face in turn.

'I think it's time we left, Mum,' Zoe said.

'What? Before you've had your cup of tea?' Mrs Bilby protested.

'We'll have it at home,' Zoe said. 'It isn't as though we've far to go.'

'Unlike me.' William stood, taking his cue from Zoe. 'This has been a very pleasant evening, thank you. I shan't wait for tea, either. I have to allow extra time for detours with all this flooding about.' He departed with an air of relief.

Having made what she considered her sensation, Mrs Rome was willing to leave. Zoe gathered up Bluebell, who knew what that meant and began purring madly while the other cats regarded her enviously.

Adolf and Enza followed them to the door and it took some fancy footwork to let the Romes out while keeping the cats in. Adolf swore and backed away as the door nearly closed on his whiskers. He stalked over to the fridge, followed by Enza, and shrieked for Danegeld. His cries brought Pasha out from the living room. Pasha looked so dejected that Bettina gave in and distributed treats to them all.

'You're spoiling those cats,' her mother said.

'The treat's on Pasha, he can afford—'

Zoe's scream ripped through the night outside.

Mrs Bilby reached the door first and wrenched it open. The cats rushed out but, for once, Bettina didn't care. Zoe was not the screaming kind, something must be terribly wrong. She left the back door wide open so that the light streamed out to illuminate their way.

'Zoe?' Bettina called. 'Zoe, where are you? What's the matter?'

'She went down to the end of the garden.' Mrs Rome shrank against her open back door, wringing her hands. 'She thought she saw something when we snapped the outdoor light on. She went down to investigate. Is she all right?'

Zoe was stumbling towards them, dripping wet and half sobbing.

'Zoe!' Bettina ran to meet her. 'What's happened?'

'Oh, God! I tripped over him!' Zoe drew a shuddering breath and fought for control as Bettina led her into the brightness and warmth of the kitchen. 'Call an ambulance! Hurry! Oh, God! I . . . I think he's dead!'

'Who?' Bettina asked.

'Nine-nine-nine!' Mrs Bilby dashed for the telephone. 'I've always wanted to ring that.'

'He was lying in a big pool of water. I fell into it when I tripped over him.' Zoe shuddered. 'He must have drowned. Oh, God! I should have tried to pull him out. At least, turned him over . . . kiss of life . . .' She shuddered again. 'I . . . I stopped thinking.'

'He'll be dead,' Mrs Rome said with grim satisfaction. 'Nothing you could do would make any difference. The cards never lie.'

'I'll take a look,' Bettina said. 'You go and change into dry clothes.'

'No, I'll come with you. I want to see it again for myself.' Zoe swallowed hard. 'Now that I'm prepared.'

'Here . . .' Mrs Rome offered her a towel.

'It doesn't matter. I'll only get wetter again.' Zoe followed Bettina down the path. As the glow from the back porch light faded behind them, a dim reflection gleamed from a Day-Glo yellow striped jacket on the ground ahead of them.

Something moved in the darkness where the figure's boots remained above the water line. Zoe gave a small shriek and halted.

'Adolf!' Bettina swooped and snatched him up. 'Come away from there! Where are the others?' She looked into the shadows – it was easier than looking at the body in the water – but nothing else was stirring.

'Bluebell's in the house.' Zoe was trying to cling to normality by focusing on mundane matters. 'And I don't think Pasha went out with the others.'

'That leaves Enza. Eeennnzzaa . . .' Bettina raised her voice, then realized she was falling into the same trap as Zoe. Enza wouldn't go far on a night like this. It was the man in the pool at their feet they had to worry about.

'Here, hold Adolf.' Bettina relinquished the warm furry body with reluctance and stooped to the cold clammy one at her feet.

He had been lying there for a long time. Too long. The jacket was sodden and slippery, the flaccid flesh beneath it seemed to send a chill through the material and there was the disquieting suggestion of a growing rigidity she could not allow herself to think about. It took several attempts before she could get a good enough grip on the shoulders to flip him over.

She was unprepared for the sudden wave washing over her feet as the body flopped back into the water. Zoe gave a muffled shriek and stepped back; she had been caught, too.

'Bettina! Zoe!' Anxious parental voices called. 'Are you all right?'

Sirens wailed in the distance, drawing closer.

'Let's go back to the house,' Zoe said. 'There's nothing we can do here. The professionals will be along in a minute. Leave it to them. Mum's right, he's beyond our help.'

It was true. The sightless eyes in the pale blob of a face stared up at the dark sky. It was hours too late for anyone to help him. All the ambulance could do would be to take him away.

'Just a few hours ago' – Zoe's voice was ragged – 'I gave

95

him a mug of coffee. And now—' Adolf gave an indignant yowl as her arms tightened suddenly.

The noise of the sirens filled the night and then stopped abruptly. A sporadic blue light flashed on the other side of the houses.

'They're here,' Bettina said. 'Let's go and meet them.'

Not even the cats could prevent them from sleeping late the next morning. Not that the cats tried; they were exhausted, too. The night had gone on for far too long and the morning had come too early.

When Bettina opened her eyes for the second time, her bedside clock said 10.30 and there was still no sound of anyone stirring anywhere in the house. She threw back the covers and got up slowly, still not feeling quite awake.

She opened the bedroom curtains and recoiled involuntarily as she looked down on the back gardens and saw the circle of trodden mud in Zoe's, marking the spot where the body had lain. The edges of the deep puddle had receded towards the centre as the saturated earth gradually reabsorbed the water. If the man had fallen face forward into that spot just twenty-four hours later, the chances were that he would have survived with nothing worse than a muddy face.

Bettina shuddered and closed the curtains again, preferring the darkened room to the view outside. She dressed quickly and paused at her mother's door on the way downstairs. With her hand on the knob, she hesitated, then incautiously turned it.

'Is that you, Bettina?'

'You're awake,' Bettina answered, repressing the temptation to ask who else her mother thought it might be. 'Are you all right?'

'I'm not too well,' her mother said. 'Last night was such a shock. I think I may stay in bed a while longer.'

'Good idea. You do that.' The relief was overwhelming; she added guiltily, 'Can I get you anything?'

'Perhaps a cup of tea, if you're making some anyway.

And a bit of toast. And I'll try to force down a poached egg – I've got to keep my strength up.'

'That's right,' Bettina agreed automatically. 'We don't want you to be ill.' She closed the door and continued downstairs.

The kitchen was dark and quiet. She risked opening the curtains and found, as she had hoped, that the hedge mercifully cut off the grim view of last night's horror.

She put the kettle on and decanted cat food into the various bowls. Enza was a furry coil of contentment in her carrier. Pasha stirred restlessly, but did not waken as she set his bowl down. One baleful green eye squinted at her from beneath the black patch of fur, then closed again; not even Adolf could be bothered to wake up and face the day. Lucky cats, they didn't have to.

The kettle began humming and a steady blast of steam issued from the spout. Bettina attended to the tea-making, then popped bread into the toaster and set an egg to poaching while the tea steeped.

Adolf yawned hugely and changed his mind about sleeping. Food – people food – was in the offing. He launched himself against the door of his carrying case and the latch, already weakened by many such assaults, was no match for him. He strolled out of the case and over to Bettina, looking up at her expectantly.

'Not now, greedy guts,' she said. 'Only what's in your bowl. That ought to be enough for any reasonable cat.'

Adolf promptly showed her how unreasonable he could be. His yowl woke the others; he heaved himself up on his hind legs, his claws lightly insinuating themselves into Bettina's knee. He repeated his demand for whatever she was cooking.

Pasha moved to the front of his case, looked at the empty spot where Bluebell's cushioned case had lain and added his complaint to Adolf's. First, Sylvia had disappeared, and now Bluebell was gone; he was alone, bereft, abandoned. The world was too miserable to be borne.

'Oh, Pasha, poor baby.' Bettina was not only sympathetic, but frightened. Despite his size – which was mostly fur – Pasha already seemed frail to the point of illness. If he should lose the will to live . . .

'Here, Pasha.' Recklessly, she slopped cod-liver oil into his saucer and unlatched the door of his carrying case. 'Cheer up. It's not as bad as it seems.'

Or was it? If Sylvia had deserted Graeme, who would get custody of Pasha? Graeme obviously didn't care about him at all – and Sylvia might have decided to leave him here, to be sent for later . . . much later. If at all . . .

Enza announced that she, too, wanted her freedom and Bettina quickly let her out, noticing that her sides seemed to have bulged out at least an extra inch overnight. Thank heavens Jack Rawson could be relied upon to return tomorrow and retrieve his little darling.

It was fortunate that the Romes had returned early; Bluebell was a sweetheart, but four cats amounted to a handful and a half in the confines of one kitchen.

Adolf yowled again and Bettina looked down at him thoughtfully. It was less fortunate that May Cassidy had decided to add another ten days on to the Bank Holiday weekend and give herself a nice long holiday with her family in Ireland. Adolf could be a handful and a half all by himself.

Of course, if one had a proper boarding cattery, with separate heated chalets for each cat and a long wired-in run where they could exercise and an assistant to help care for them and—

'BETTINA! BETTINA!' Her mother's shrill voice broke in on the pleasant reverie. 'Hasn't that kettle boiled yet? What's taking so long?'

'Just ready now, Mother,' she called back, swiftly assembling the tea tray and starting for the door. She glanced back in time to see Adolf and Enza executing a pincer movement on Pasha, shouldering him aside and zeroing in on his cod-liver oil.

She was halfway up the stairs when the doorbell rang

an abrupt, peremptory summons. She halted irresolutely for a moment, the tray teetering in her hands.

'Doorbell, Bettina.'

'I hear it.' She resumed climbing the stairs. 'I'll answer it in a minute.'

'Is that my tea?' Her mother appeared at the head of the stairs. 'There's a police car out front. If that's the police, don't let them in.'

'If it's the police, I'll have to let them in.' Bettina surrendered the tray and went back downstairs. The doorbell sounded urgently again.

'All right, I'm coming!' she shouted, aware of her mother's disapproving gaze.

'What is it?' She swung back the door, still not in the best of moods.

'Good morning, Mrs Bilby.' Two men stood there. The older man was not in uniform, the constable beside him was.

'I'm *Miss* Bilby,' she found herself snapping.

'Sorry, Miss Bilby.' The plain-clothes man swung a small card in front of her eyes, too quickly to be read. 'I'm sorry to disturb you so early but—'

'Is that the police?' her mother demanded loudly from the top of the stairs.

'That's right, madam.' The man stepped forward, a practised public relations smile on his lips. 'Just a matter of routine . . .'

'If you have to let them in,' Mrs Bilby said, 'make sure you count the spoons before they leave.'

The smile congealed on his face.

'I'm so sorry,' Bettina apologized quickly, abysmally aware that it would do no good. 'You mustn't mind my mother. She's a bit difficult . . . at times.'

'We've heard worse than that,' the man said. 'These days.' And he was prepared to forgive none of it.

'Please' – Bettina stepped back – 'do come in.'

'Are you sure you wouldn't like to lock up the silver first?'

'I've said I'm sorry.' A trace of asperity crept into her voice. 'I really can't be held responsible for my mother's opinions. And' — she added a bit of nastiness on her own account — 'it *was* all over the local newspaper.'

'This week it will be in the nationals. They pick up anything that's too good to miss.' His tone was bleak and, for a moment, his faint air of dejection was so like Pasha's that her heart softened.

'Would you like a cup of tea?' she offered, leading them into the living room. 'Or coffee — if you don't mind instant?'

'No, thank you.' The older man established his rank by answering for them both without a glance at his uniformed constable.

The cats marched in from the kitchen on a tour of inspection. They, too, ignored the constable, and circled the older man warily.

'Do sit down,' Bettina said. 'I'm sorry, I didn't get your name . . . ?'

'Inspector Hughes.' He did not introduce the constable, who perched on the edge of a chair while the inspector chose the sofa, leaning forward and offering his hand to be sniffed. Adolf and Pasha kept their distance, but Enza, certain of her welcome from all susceptible males, sniffed delicately at the hand and then leaped into his lap.

'She must smell Timmy on me,' he said with a trace of complacency as he began to stroke her.

'Timmy is your cat?' Bettina was aware that she was beginning to unbend. Even if he was from a highly suspect station house, a policeman with a cat couldn't be all bad.

'Timon of Athens,' he said, half defiantly. 'A Siamese.'

'How lovely!' The exclamation was so heartfelt that he thawed.

'He is, rather. That is—' With a swift sideways glance at the constable, he cleared his throat and became more formal. 'This little lady seems to think so. Like to meet my Timmy, would you?'

Enza purred agreement, rubbing her head against the friendly hand.

'She'd better wait until she's discharged her duty to Adolf,' Bettina said.

'Ah, yes.' The hands stroked Enza's sides assessingly. 'Another two or three weeks perhaps?'

'About that.'

'And this must be Adolf.' He looked down into the jealous eyes at knee level, glaring at him. 'Well named, isn't he? Striking markings.'

'Just wait until you hear him haranguing the rabble. Then you'll really know how he earned his name. May Cassidy always did have a wild sense of humour.'

'Oh? He's not yours, then?' The quick look of interest swung to her from the cats.

'None of them are, I'm sorry to say. I don't have a cat of my own. I just seem to have fallen into the position of neighbourhood cat-sitter to everyone else's pets.'

'And yet' – he met her eyes in one keen glance that veered away and returned to the cats almost as soon as she'd noticed it – 'you're so fond of them.'

'Yes, but my mother—' She broke off.

'Ah, yes.' He glanced ceilingwards. 'Quite.'

Bettina could hear sounds of activity overhead, which presaged an imminent appearance. The one thing her mother had in common with the cats was a curiosity that would not be denied.

'You wanted to ask some questions?' Bettina spoke hurriedly. If she could speed up this conversation, perhaps they might get it over with before her mother came downstairs. 'It's about the accident to the Water Board man last night, I suppose?' There was a creak on the stairs. Bettina cast a harried glance towards the doorway, one which became even more harried as she realized that, having broken all records getting dressed, her mother was now going to stand outside in the hallway and eavesdrop.

'Shall we wait until your mother arrives?' Inspector Hughes was no fool. 'Then we shan't have to ask the same questions twice.' He stared pointedly at the doorway, but it remained empty.

'I'll just go and see—' Bettina began. He stopped her with an abrupt gesture.

'Please come in.' Inspector Hughes raised his voice. 'We're waiting for you, madam.'

'Humph!' Mrs Bilby appeared in the doorway and swept them with a withering look, clearly unimpressed and letting them know it. 'So they're still here!'

'We haven't finished our inquiries, madam.' Inspector Hughes remained seated, firmly anchored by Enza, who had settled down on his lap. At least, Bettina divined, that was his ostensible excuse; it was also more than possible that he had not forgiven Mrs Bilby her earlier remark and saw no reason to extend any courtesies to her. Her present attitude wasn't going to ease the situation, either. The inspector sent a sharp glance towards the constable, who had risen to his feet and the unfortunate young man dropped back into his chair, his face turning bright pink.

'I don't know why you have to make any inquiries here,' Mrs Bilby said. 'That stupid man drowned in the Romes' garden, not ours. You should be next door talking to them.'

'We'll get to them, madam. I understand the deceased and another man had been in every garden in the vicinity yesterday afternoon. Do you know why they—'

'Because the Water Board is staffed by a pack of incompetent idiots!' Mrs Bilby could not wait for the end of the question to enlighten him. 'None of them can remember where they've put their drains. Every time we looked out of the windows yesterday – front or back – there were fools splashing about in puddles. It's a wonder more of them haven't drowned.'

Adolf voiced a sudden opinion as to someone he would

like to see drowned. Mrs Bilby glared at him and he glared back.

'We're trying to trace his movements during the day. Could either of you tell us what time he was here?'

'You're not a local man,' Mrs Bilby accused suddenly. 'You have a different accent – a country accent.'

'That's right,' Inspector Hughes said. 'I'm from the West Sussex Constabulary. A group of us from different regions have been seconded to your local station to make up for the suspensions. Not enough, though. The station is still short-staffed and fully stretched, but we're doing our best. If you could kindly answer the questions, it would help us a great deal.'

'Helping with inquiries!' Mrs Bilby said. 'We all know what that means. Do you suspect' – her eyes gleamed – 'foul play?'

'In this case, it means just what it says.' He gave her a jaded look. 'We are simply trying to establish what happened. The man was dead when the ambulance arrived and the accident report has to have a routine follow-up.'

'They were here most of the afternoon,' Bettina said. 'In one back garden or another. Most of the neighbours are away for the holiday, so they were able to poke about without interference. They – the man who died – came to our back door sometime about half past three and wanted to come in and check the roof, but Mother wouldn't let him in.'

'Check the roof, indeed!' Mrs Bilby sniffed. 'What would the Water Board be doing with the roof? Burglars, that's what they were! They didn't fool *me!* Wanted to look around and see what was worth stealing, so that they could come back later and get it. The police ought to be watching out for suspicious characters like that – if they weren't too busy doing their own thieving!'

'Mother!' Bettina protested automatically.

'Then only one of them came to the back door?' Inspector Hughes ignored Mrs Bilby's outburst. 'Where was the other man?'

'He was waiting at the bottom of the garden,' Bettina said.

'Did you hear either of them call the other by name?'

'You mean you don't even know who he is?' Mrs Bilby's nod said she had expected no better. 'Why not? Wouldn't the Water Board tell you?'

'He wasn't carrying any identification,' Inspector Hughes said patiently, conveying the implication that he would answer reasonable questions, but would not deal with hysterical nonsense about burglars.

'And we haven't been able to get through to the Water Board yet. They're trying to deal with all the storm emergencies and they've put a recorded message on their phone line. Someone else has gone round to call on them personally.'

'If there's anyone there,' Mrs Bilby said. 'The lazy—'

'Or everyone is out on emergency work,' Bettina said quickly; Inspector Hughes was getting that jaded look again. 'Even some of the higher-ups were trying to unblock a drain out front earlier in the day.'

'They weren't very good at it,' Mrs Bilby said, 'but it did my heart good to see them get their Savile Row suits soaking wet. It was probably the first time they'd ever sullied their hands in their whole miserable, useless lives.'

'Anyway, we didn't hear any names,' Bettina said. 'You should ask Zoe Rome next door. She might know. She was talking to them and even gave them mugs of coffee.'

'Zoe is a fool!' Mrs Bilby said. 'So is her mother. Anyone could talk those women out of anything!'

'Perhaps it would be best to speak to them.' Inspector Hughes, holding Enza, rose to his feet. 'If we have any more questions . . .' He sent Mrs Bilby an inscrutable look.

'I'll be back at work tomorrow,' Bettina said. 'At Jelwyn Accessories. I'm personal assistant to Mr Norris—'

'We called them secretaries in my day,' Mrs Bilby sniffed. 'They didn't get so above themselves then.'

The constable was already at the door, anxious to escape. Inspector Hughes transferred Enza to Bettina's arms, giving her a look that told her he had correctly interpreted her message and would arrange to speak to her at the office without constant interruptions from her mother if it became necessary to ask any further questions.

'Good riddance!' Mrs Bilby said, before the door had quite closed behind them. 'All tarred with the same brush, they are. Give them enough time to learn their way around these parts and they'll be in it up to their armpits, too.'

Bettina watched the ramrod-stiff backs of the two men marching down the path; they had heard every word, no doubt about it. As Mrs Bilby had intended them to.

Bettina was conscious of a ghostlike echo from her childhood: *'I'll never see them again.'* Friends she had brought home from school to play who, having encountered Mrs Bilby, never returned. They had remained friendly enough but wary, and all contact with them had thenceforward been on their territory. It had not been long before she had learned not to invite anyone home . . .

'Are you going to stand there all day?' her mother demanded. 'I didn't get the chance to have my breakfast with those people here and everything will be cold now. I can't drink cold tea – and cold poached egg is disgusting!'

'The cats will eat it,' Bettina said. 'I'll chop it up for them.'

'The cats! The cats! The cats! What about me?'

'I'll put the kettle on.' Bettina turned away from the door, still wondering at the faint sense of loss she felt.

Mrs Bilby had retired for her afternoon nap when Zoe tapped at the back door and entered quickly, before the cats could get out. She was carrying a small covered roasting pan, holding it a good distance away from her.

'Have you,' she asked, too sweetly, 'anything you'd like to tell me?'

'Oh, dear! I was hoping you wouldn't find it until I had a chance to speak to you about it,' Bettina said.

'It's a good job I'm the one who found it. We'd have had a prize case of hysteria on our hands if Mum had uncovered it.' Zoe set the pan on the table and stared at her accusingly. 'What on earth are you playing at?'

Adolf caught the scent and leaped for the table top.

'Oh, no, you don't!' Bettina caught him up and tossed him back to the floor. His paws hardly touched it before he rebounded to the table top.

Pasha strolled over to see what was going on, Enza was right behind him. Adolf let out a cry for reinforcements and Pasha jumped on to the table.

'For heaven's sake!' Bettina snatched up the roasting pan and thrust it at Zoe. 'Take this away. Put it back. Please. They're getting overexcited.'

'So am I,' Zoe said. 'Why should I put this . . . this *thing* . . . back into *my* deepfreeze? Why can't you put it in yours?'

'Because if *my* mother finds it—'

'Why don't you just throw it away?'

'Because— Stop that!' Adolf was teetering on the edge of the table, striking out with his paw, trying to knock the pan from her hands.

'Distract them,' Zoe said. She reached up to the shelf above the table and tossed a handful of cat treats to the floor.

Enza promptly began eating them. Pasha dropped to the floor and dived in for his share. Adolf fixed Bettina with a baleful eye – there was more than cat treats around here and he wanted it. Meanwhile . . . he jumped to the floor and jostled the others aside.

'Now,' Zoe said. 'Why have you suddenly become so attached to a dead pigeon?'

'BETTINA!' her mother called. 'Who are you talking to? Have those policemen come back?'

'No, Mother, it's only Zoe.' Bettina went out to the foot of the stairs. 'Go back to sleep.'

'Sleep! Sleep! As though anyone could get any rest around here. There's never a quiet moment.' There was the sound of feet hitting the floor heavily. 'I might as well get up.'

'She's coming down.' Bettina rushed back into the kitchen and pushed the roasting pan at Zoe. 'Take this back. Please. If she sees it again, I'll never hear the end of it. Please. Put it back. I'll explain later.'

'And what about *my* mother? Oh, all right.' Zoe took the pan with ill grace. 'I'll hide it under the broccoli. She hates that, so she'd never touch it.'

The middle stair creaked loudly. Zoe opened the back door and darted out. Bettina sank weakly into a chair, limp with relief.

Abruptly, she felt a sneeze coming on and snatched automatically for the paper handkerchief in her pocket. As she pulled it out, she was suddenly aware that something else had come out with it; something that curved in a glittering arc from the fold of the handkerchief to the floor.

Sneeze forgotten, she lurched forward to retrieve it. Too late. Adolf pounced, gulping at it.

'No, Adolf! No!' She grabbed at him.

He backed away swiftly and gave her a defiant look. Then there was the telltale muscle movement of his throat as he swallowed.

'No! No!' She was on her knees beside him, pleading. 'No, you can't! Spit it out. Come on.' She began patting him vigorously on the back. 'Cough it up!'

'Bettina! What are you doing?'

'Adolf—' Bettina said. 'Adolf—' She could not explain.

Adolf gave a choking wheeze and backed farther away, looking as though he might be having second thoughts about that last cat treat.

'That cat isn't going to be sick, is he?'

'I hope so.'

'What?'

'I'm afraid Adolf has just swallowed . . . a stone.'

'Greedy monster!' Mrs Bilby was untroubled by the news. She was more upset by the state of the floor. 'That

108

Zoe has been tracking in mud again. I wish that girl would learn to wipe her feet on the mat. You'd think she'd been brought up in a barn.'

Adolf sauntered over to the water bowl and settled down for a long drinking session. Bettina watched him anxiously.

'Don't worry about that cat,' her mother said. 'He's tougher than you are. A little stone isn't going to bother him. It will come out all right at the end.' She gave one of her rare barks of laughter at her own joke.

Yes, and Adolf would require close supervision to make sure that it did. Bettina's fingers explored the two loose stones remaining in her pocket. Both had sharp pointed ends. That meant Adolf had swallowed the emerald cut. Of them all, it was the safest for him, with no sharp point to pierce his intestines. There was a sporting chance it would make its way through his system without doing him any harm.

'I'll give him some cod-liver oil,' Bettina decided. 'That should help ease it through.'

'Castor oil would be better.'

'We don't have any – and I doubt that he'd take it. Perhaps I should call the vet.'

'We're not running up any vet's bills! If May Cassidy feels she can afford them, she can call the vet when she gets back. It's only a few more days. Surely the cat can last until then.'

Adolf finished drinking, hiccoughed, and retreated a few paces to sit down and begin washing his face. He seemed all right . . . so far.

'Here, Adolf.' Bettina poured a dollop of cod-liver oil into a saucer and set it down in front of him. Then, noticing Pasha's injured look, poured more into a separate saucer for him. Enza promptly began licking at it from the opposite side of the saucer and it developed into a race for Pasha to get his fair share.

'*That's* the cat you ought to be worrying about.' Mrs Bilby indicated Pasha. 'We're being *paid* to take care of *him*.'

The money was actually for Pasha's food and cod-liver oil, but Bettina knew better than to argue with her mother who was falling into a moderately good mood at the thought of the extra cash.

What would Mrs Bilby do if she knew about the diamonds? Unidentifiable ... untraceable. Could she be trusted not to try to appropriate them for her own use? It was better not to risk the arguments. Especially now that Adolf had swallowed one of them. There had always been a certain ring in her mother's voice when she read out the bedtime story about killing the goose that laid the golden eggs which suggested she felt her own technique with a carving knife might have achieved the hoped-for result.

No, Adolf had brought enough trouble on himself without adding that. He still looked fine, however, and seemed to be breathing normally. Judging from the way he was gulping down the cod-liver oil, he was having no difficulty swallowing, nor was his throat sore. He might just get away with it.

'I'll keep Adolf in my room tonight,' Bettina decided. 'I can watch him and, if he seems to be having any problems, I can call the vet then.'

'You're a fool over those cats! Don't say I didn't warn you.'

By nightfall, Adolf was the happiest cat in the house. An afternoon of being cuddled in Bettina's lap, followed every time he moved away, and constantly caressed, had convinced him that he was Top Cat and was finally being shown the favouritism he deserved. He was not to know that the stroking fingers were probing gently at his abdomen, trying to discover the progress of the diamond through his intestinal tract.

It was useless, though; she couldn't feel a thing. Adolf was too well muscled, too padded, too furred; his secrets were his own.

Enza had curled up on the sofa next to Mrs Bilby, who

was condescending to pat her occasionally as she watched television. Pasha was sunk in dejection as he enviously watched the stroking fingers. Even Mrs Bilby noticed.

'You ought to be paying more attention to Pasha,' she said during a commercial break. 'He's the valuable cat.'

Little did she know. Bettina forced a smile.

'Worth his weight in diamonds,' Mrs Bilby quoted derisively.

Adolf yelped as the probing fingers dug in suddenly.

The telephone rang and Bettina started up. 'Zoe, probably,' she told her mother. 'I'll answer it.'

'Can you talk?' Zoe asked without preamble.

'Not really.'

'Oh, too bad. Mine's gone to bed. I thought possibly—'

'Television,' Bettina said briefly. 'The Noël Coward season started tonight. She's watching.'

'So am I. Off and on. Shall we meet for lunch tomorrow? We can talk then.'

'Yes. No!' Bettina abruptly realized that she could not go to work in the morning. Not unless Adolf had delivered himself of the diamond. She was going to have to stay within monitoring range until Adolf had excreted the gem.

'Look,' Bettina said. 'I can't explain now, but something's come up – or gone down,' she corrected with a mirthless laugh. 'I'm not going to work tomorrow, perhaps not for a couple of days. I'll ring you when I get a chance and we can—'

'You mean I have to keep that *thing* in my freezer indefinitely? That can't be sanitary. There must be all kinds of health regulations against it. Why don't you—'

'Sorry.' Bettina was conscious of a shadow beyond the glass of the front door. 'Someone's at the door. I'll talk to you later. Maybe tomorrow.' She hung up just as the bell rang.

'I'll get it,' she called to her mother, who had no intention of moving. She released the guard chain as she recognized the caller and swung the door open.

'Good evening, Graeme,' she said. 'Had any luck finding Sylvia?'

'Not really.' Graeme stepped inside and looked around sharply, as though he expected to find Sylvia lurking in the shadows. 'I went down to Erith and talked to her aunt, but she hadn't seen or heard from her in weeks. I had the devil of a time getting away – and she was no help at all.'

'Sorry to hear that.'

'You're sure you haven't heard from her?' He stared at Bettina intently, as though seeking to catch her out in some lie.

'Not a word.' Bettina felt a faint stir of indignation. 'Why should I?'

'Pasha,' he said. 'She wouldn't have gone away and left Pasha. That is,' he corrected himself, 'not for long. She was planning to collect him from you in the morning. I thought she might have telephoned to change the arrangement – or, at least, ask how he is.'

'Well, she hasn't. I'm sorry, Graeme, but—'

'Bettina!' her mother called. 'Who's out there?'

'It's just Graeme, Mother. He's still looking for Sylvia.'

'Well, he'd better look somewhere else. She still isn't here.'

Pasha appeared in the doorway, drawn by the familiar voice. He stared at Graeme and moved forward to circle him warily, sniffing at his shoes. He, too, was looking for Sylvia.

'Poor baby,' Bettina said. 'He misses her dreadfully.'

'As well he might.' Graeme looked down at Pasha without affection. 'No one else will ever spoil him the way she does.'

Pasha gave a despairing little cry and retreated back to the living room. Mrs Bilby greeted him with a remark that was inaudible but clearly uncomplimentary.

Adolf sauntered into the hallway with a faintly arrogant air; it had been a whole five minutes since his last cuddle, his new slave was falling down on the job.

'All these cats.' Graeme glanced at him. 'I hope they're not too destructive.'

'They're very well behaved,' Bettina said, just as Adolf began sharpening his claws on the stair carpet.

'You shouldn't have much trouble with Pasha.' Graeme stared into her eyes earnestly. 'He couldn't catch a mouse or a bird if you put it in his mouth for him. He isn't good for much of anything, in fact.'

'Poor Pasha.' Bettina wondered if Graeme and Sylvia had quarrelled over the cat, if that had something to do with her disappearance. 'He has his problems.'

'Not half as many as he's given us,' Graeme complained. 'We have three people threatening law suits for return of their stud fees. They're not entitled, of course. Pasha covered their queens without any difficulty. It's just that there weren't any results. These things happen sometimes.'

Bettina nodded sympathetically. They were happening too often with Pasha and word was getting round. Was it possible that her mother was right and Sylvia had decided to cut *all* her losses – unsatisfactory cat as well as unsatisfactory husband?

'If you should hear from Sylvia,' Graeme said nervously, 'you *will* let me know?'

'Of course.' Bettina tried to sound reassuring. 'But I'm sure you'll hear before I will.'

'Yes.' He nodded, but still seemed reluctant to leave, looking around anxiously again. 'There's been some sort of ridiculous mix-up. We'll get it sorted out.'

Bettina was asleep, a contented Adolf curled against the small of her back, when a deeper, louder purr disturbed her dreams and made her stir uneasily. She didn't wake, but something deep in her unconscious mind followed the sound of a heavy motor cruising past the house, down to the end of the street, back again, and over to the next street. Up and down . . . up and down . . .

CHAPTER 11

'Bettina! Bettina! You'll be late for work.' Her mother rattled the doorknob, thwarted at finding the door locked. 'Bettina! Are you all right?'

'Yes, yes, I'm coming.' Ignoring Adolf's protests, Bettina threw back the covers and stumbled to the door, unlocking it and throwing it open.

'You locked your door!' Mrs Bilby accused.

'If I don't, it springs open sometimes,' Bettina defended. 'I didn't want Adolf to get out.'

'Blasted cat!' Mrs Bilby regarded Adolf without favour as he fought his way free of the covers and stretched luxuriously. 'You'd better worry more about yourself and less about him. What will you do if you lose your job? Hurry up or you'll be really late.'

'I'm not going in today,' Bettina said. 'I – I don't feel too well. I'll ring up and tell them.'

'What's wrong?' Her mother looked at her sharply.

'Oh, I don't know.' She couldn't tell the truth: *I can't leave Adolf.* That would really send her mother berserk.

'My head aches . . . and I feel terribly tired . . . sort of drained . . .' It wasn't really a lie, even as she spoke a vague malaise came over her. It would be so nice to go back to bed, back to sleep, and leave the world and all its problems for someone else to face. She sighed and drooped, without realizing she was doing so.

'I hope you're not coming down with something. After all that running around in the wet gardens, it wouldn't surprise me a bit. You're old enough to know better.'

'There wasn't much else I could do.' Her mother spoke

114

as though finding a dead body was something that could be ignored until the weather improved.

'Perhaps not.' Her mother suddenly looked indecisive. 'Do you want to go back to bed? Shall I bring you a cup of tea?' She must really be worried.

'Thanks, but I'll get dressed and come downstairs. I'm not that bad, I'm just not bright enough to face a full day at the office.' Particularly not when there wasn't a full day's work there to occupy her; but, if she admitted that, her mother's worries would only increase. It was best not to let her suspect that the firm was faltering.

Adolf leaped from the bed and strolled purposefully towards the open door. Bettina checked quickly; he had not used the litter tray during the night.

'Don't let him out!' She moved quickly, darting around her mother and slamming the door just before Adolf reached it. He halted and glared at her, affronted.

'Really!' Her mother was scarcely less affronted. 'What on earth . . . ?'

'I don't want him out of my sight. Not until I'm sure he's going to be all right.'

Adolf sat down with his back to them and stared pointedly at the door. After a moment, he uttered a loud cry of complaint.

'Oh, no, you don't!' Bettina picked him up, still protesting. 'You'll go downstairs when I do.' She added to her mother, hoping she'd take the hint: 'I'll get dressed now and be right down.'

'I'll go and put the kettle on then.' Her mother gave Adolf an old-fashioned look and went out of the room quickly, while he tried to struggle free from Bettina's embrace.

'Not yet, you don't.' She set him down firmly in the litter tray. 'Now *try!*'

He glared at her and stepped out of the tray, shaking each paw fastidiously and complaining again. He didn't know what her problem was, but she was getting no cooperation from him.

After breakfast, Bettina called Mr Norris and, in a weak voice, explained that she wasn't feeling well and might be in tomorrow . . . if she improved.

'Take your time,' Mr Norris said gloomily. 'There won't be much business transacted this week. Too many people are busy mopping up after the storm. Do you still have your electricity?'

'It went out the first night, but we got it back in the morning. After that, it flickered a few times, but we didn't lose it again.'

'You're lucky. Ours went on Saturday night and we haven't got it back yet. I'm taking Lucy to lunch – she's desperate for a proper cooked meal – and I'll probably take the rest of the day off and go home with her. She doesn't like being alone in the house without any light or central heating. Thank God for the fireplaces. We were able to cook sausages and toast on forks. Between that and the wine cellar, we made it through the weekend.'

He was considerably more cheerful when he rang off. Bettina recognized that the telling of the What-Did-You-Do-in-the-Great-Storm? story was going to brighten the post-holiday letdown for the next few days whenever people met. It was too bad she wouldn't be able to relate her own experiences.

She felt more cheerful herself as she went back into the living room; it was perfectly true that the outside world was not going to get back to normal for some time. In an obscure way, that seemed to extend her absolution from the immediate necessity to do anything about the diamonds.

Also, there was the added complication of Adolf. Even if she should discover the owner of the gems, she could not hand over most of the diamonds – and someone else's cat. The stone Adolf had swallowed was one of the largest; she had an uneasy suspicion that its value was in the tens of thousands. If she couldn't get it back from Adolf, she might be accused of stealing it for herself. If she ever found the right person to give it back to.

116

'Where's Adolf?' she asked abruptly. None of the cats were in the living room.

'I hope you don't expect me to keep track of those cats. It's bad enough—'

'You didn't let them out!' Bettina started for the kitchen.

'No, I didn't! That Adolf was agitating to go out for all he was worth, though. Cheeky little monkey!' Mrs Bilby's tone betrayed the fact that her sole reason for not letting them out was to thwart Adolf. If he hadn't wanted to go out, she'd have swept him out in a minute.

Pasha came to meet Bettina hopefully.

'Good boy.' She gave him a perfunctory pat. 'Where's Adolf?'

Pasha turned away as though he had expected nothing better and went to sit beside his empty food dish, staring at it glumly.

'Adolf?' She looked around anxiously, fighting down a pang of guilt about Pasha. He was feeling neglected, he was *being* neglected. She must find time to give him some attention, but she couldn't lose sight of Adolf.

'Adolf?' she called again. He was nowhere in sight, but she knew how to smoke him out. It would cheer Pasha, too. She took down the box of cat treats and, rattling them noisily, poured some into each bowl.

The curtains at the window moved and Adolf emerged from behind them. Enza came out of her carrying case. Pasha brightened.

'What's outside?' Bettina remembered the last time Adolf had been so engrossed in the scene from the kitchen window. Had he actually seen the man fall into the puddle and drown? Or had he simply known that the body was there? Rather nervously, she went over to the window to look out.

All seemed peaceful and quiet out there. The ground had absorbed most of the water but still looked spongy and muddy. The hedge was too thick to see through to the other side, but she knew the view would be the same, except for the footprints in the mud surrounding the spot where the man had lain.

She shuddered and turned away from the window, back into the warm domesticity of the kitchen where the cats had now finished their treats and were watching her hopefully for more.

'Not right now,' she said. Adolf screamed a protest, but the others accepted the decision philosophically.

'BETTINA!' her mother called. 'There's someone at the door.' To prove it, the doorbell rang.

'I'll get it.'

'It's that nosey woman again,' her mother reported from behind the living room curtain. 'What does she want now?'

'I'm most dreadfully sorry to disturb you.' Vivien Smythe gave a nervous smile as Bettina opened the door. 'I feel so silly. Really, I *do* apologize but— I *do* hope you can help me. Er, do you mind if I come in?'

'Oh, sorry.' Bettina backed away, suddenly aware that she had been blocking the doorway.

'Thanks awfully.' Vivien stepped into the hallway, her voice rising with a nervous quaver. 'You see, when I was here the other day . . . When I was *somewhere* – I can't be sure it was here – I'm afraid I lost one of the charms from my bracelet. It has a deeply sentimental value for me. So, I'm having to retrace my steps to every place I've visited during the past few days.' She swept a hand across her forehead distractedly. 'I feel such an idiot.'

'What a shame.' Bettina followed Vivien, who was striding into the living room as she spoke. 'But I'm afraid I haven't seen—'

'Oh, but you haven't been *looking* for it, have you? You wouldn't have noticed something that had rolled under a chair or fallen into a corner.'

'No,' Bettina admitted, 'perhaps not.' Heaven knew she had had far greater things to worry about than what might be lurking under the furniture.

'Humph!' Mrs Bilby said.

118

'Oh!' Vivien shied back, then took a deep breath and stood her ground. 'Hello. I was just explaining to your daughter—'

'I heard you.' Mrs Bilby's severe gaze implied that she didn't believe a word of it.

'Yes . . . well . . . I'm sorry to be such a nuisance, but if I could just have a look around, I'd be most eternally grateful.' She bared her teeth in what was meant to be a conciliatory smile. 'Honestly, I would.'

'Look all you please,' Mrs Bilby said. 'You won't find anything here.'

'Oh, thanks.' Vivien began stalking around the room at a half-crouch, stooping lower as she passed items of furniture. 'Of course, it might have been kicked into another room. You wouldn't have noticed it, it's so small. Or the cats might have found it and begun playing with it and carried it off to anywhere in the house—'

'*Humph!*'

'Yes, well . . .' Vivien looked desperately unhappy. 'Stranger things have happened. You never can tell.'

They couldn't, indeed. Bettina was beginning to feel that she was becoming an expert on the strange byways Life could suddenly lurch down. Not the least of which was to find a designer-clad alleged market researcher practically demanding to be allowed to search her house.

'Nonsense!' Fortunately, her mother was more than a match for the interloper. 'I never heard such nonsense in my life!'

'It's got to be *somewhere*,' Vivien said. 'I'm sure I had it when I came to this house.'

'And you had it with you when you left this house,' Mrs Bilby declared. 'You were roaming up and down the streets around here all day; it probably dropped off and fell in the gutter.' The thought seemed to please her. 'With all this rain, it was probably sluiced down a drain and carried away. You'll never find it now.'

'But I've *got* to!' Vivien seemed on the point of bursting into tears. 'It means everything to me. It's an artist's palette, complete with little brushes – my father gave it to me when I graduated from the Slade.'

'Oh, Mother!' It was too much if she was going to begin scolding strangers. Bettina turned to Vivien apologetically, at the same time realizing that the woman was more believable as an artist than as a market researcher. 'I'm sorry—'

'Oh!' Vivien was paying no attention, she had been distracted by something on the far side of the room. 'It's that beautiful cat again! I've been thinking about him.'

Pasha had appeared in the kitchen doorway with Adolf and Enza. Drawn by the sound of a new voice, they had come to see what they might be missing.

Pasha lifted his head, catching the note of admiration in the cooing voice, so like the one he knew. He strutted forward, sure of his welcome as Vivien stooped to greet him.

'Who's a beautiful baby?' she crooned. 'Who's a great big gorgeous boy? Do you remember me?'

Pasha hurled himself against the outstretched hand. He closed his eyes, inhaling the rich heady perfume, he stroked his whiskers against the hem of the cashmere cape and burst into loud impassioned purrs.

'I think he does know me!' Vivien looked up with shining eyes. 'I think he likes me!'

'That cat is a snob,' Mrs Bilby said. 'He never acts like that with *me*.'

And she never treated him as Vivien was treating him: talking softly and admiringly, praising him, smoothing the long silken fur. Pasha was in his element. He surged up on his hind legs, planting his forepaws on her knees and cried to be picked up and cuddled.

Vivien responded instantly, sweeping him into her arms, burying her face in his fur. 'Oh, he's so lovely!'

'Pity he's useless,' Mrs Bilby said.

'What use does he have to be?' Vivien sprang to his defence. 'He's like a work of art – it would be enough just to be able to look at him. But he's a living work of art that can respond, give back the love one wants simply to shower on him . . .' There was a pause while she and Pasha rubbed faces enthusiastically.

'Humph!' Mrs Bilby eyed them both without favour. 'That's what you'd be like, if I let you,' she accused Bettina. 'Making a fool of yourself over a cat.'

Adolf had been watching jealously. Now he head-butted Bettina's ankles, demanding to be picked up and given his share of affection. Bettina stooped and complied.

That left Enza odd cat out. She gave Mrs Bilby a measuring look and obviously didn't rate her chances. She sat down and began a leisurely and thorough bath.

'Where's the other beautiful cat?' Vivien asked. 'The other longhair?'

'Bluebell went home, thank God,' Mrs Bilby said. 'Her owners came back early and collected her. That's one less nuisance around the place.'

'Oh?' Vivien was suddenly, elaborately casual. 'Took her back where? Do they live around here?'

'Next door,' Mrs Bilby said. 'And that's too close. Bluebell's around here half the time as it is.'

'Yes, yes, that *is* close.' Vivien looked thoughtful. 'I think I ought to talk to them.'

'Don't be silly,' Mrs Bilby said. 'Your charm couldn't possibly be over there. You were never there in the first place.'

'That's what I meant.' Vivien began speaking rapidly. 'My brief was to interview every family in the area. They weren't here before, so I couldn't. Now that they're back, I ought to fill in a form for them.'

'But you've already filled out their form,' Bettina said. 'Don't you remember? Zoe came back while you were here and you said you could kill two birds with—' She broke off. Suddenly she felt it unwise to mention birds.

'You said "they".' Vivien had a calculating glint in her eyes that had not been there before. 'I didn't interview both of them, did I?'

'No,' Bettina admitted. 'Only Zoe. Mrs Rome didn't come over then.'

'I thought not. I'm sure I ought to speak to the other occupant of the house. I'll just—' Vivien bent to deposit Pasha on the floor. 'Oh!'

Pasha had extended his claws and hooked them firmly in her cape. He was not ready to end this happy encounter. He gazed at her reproachfully.

'Here, let me help.' Bettina set Adolf down and gently unhooked Pasha's claws and smoothed the material. 'I don't think he's pulled any threads.'

Pasha gave an agonized wail.

'Oh, poor baby.' Vivien bent and stroked him. 'I don't want to leave you, but I really must.' She gave Bettina a small apologetic smile. 'Duty calls.'

'It might be a good idea to wait until later,' Bettina told her. 'Zoe will be back from the library then. If you have any more questions, she can answer them better than her mother can.'

'Her mother will read you the answers from the tea leaves,' Mrs Bilby prophesied grimly. 'Or perhaps the cards. They're both about as reliable.'

'Oh, er.' Vivien hesitated, irresolute. 'When will . . . Zoe . . . be back from work?'

'About six o'clock, I think. Unless it's one of her late nights, then it will be closer to nine.'

'Oh, that's no good at all,' Vivien said. 'I mean, I finish work at five.'

'I see,' Bettina said. She saw that Vivien seemed to have forgotten how badly she needed overtime.

'I'll just have to interview the person who *is* at home,' Vivien said.

'Well, don't blame us if you get some silly answers,' Mrs Bilby said.

'I won't.' Vivien started for the door, Pasha trailing her. 'But, if they're too unsatisfactory, perhaps I could make an appointment and come back another day.'

'You do that,' Mrs Bilby said drily.

'I hope you find your charm,' Bettina said.

'Yes, well, thank you. It's been most kind of you. If you *do* happen to find my charm, perhaps you could let me know.' She pulled a piece of paper from her handbag and scrawled a telephone number on one corner, tore it off carefully and handed it to Bettina.

'We will.' Bettina accepted the scrap of paper and shut the front door behind Vivien. She glanced down at it as she returned to the living room and was not surprised to see that it was a central London number.

Reflectively, she straightened a chair, then paused and looked behind it.

'What are you looking for?' her mother asked.

'Vivien's charm—' She broke off.

'Don't tell me you believed a word of that!'

'No,' Bettina said thoughtfully. 'No, I don't believe I did.'

Pasha leaped onto the windowsill and stared wistfully after the departing figure.

CHAPTER 12

Just after two o'clock, the telephone rang and Bettina answered.

'Hello?' She waited, but there was no response. 'Hello?'

After a long moment, the receiver at the other end was replaced.

'Who is it?' her mother called.

'Wrong number,' she replied, hoping she was right.

She hurried back to the kitchen just in time to see Adolf raise himself up in the litter box and delicately begin to bury something. She rushed over and lifted Adolf out of the way to inspect what he had done. There was just a wet patch on the kitty litter. Nothing else.

Adolf squirmed and demanded to be put down. Once down, he stalked a good distance away before turning and regarding her with the jaundiced look of a cat who was beginning to decide that there was such a thing as *too* much attention.

'Good Adolf,' she cooed. 'Nice Adolf. Why don't we give you a bit more cod-liver oil, Adolf?'

It was going to be a long day.

'Bettina!' her mother called. 'Those men are back again – and they're coming here.'

Bettina abandoned the teapot she had been filling and returned to the living room to join her mother behind the curtains. Sure enough, there were the men they had last seen splashing about in the flooded area down the street. They were somewhat more suitably dressed today, but the suits were still of an expensive cut and the patrician air of the silver haired, older man suggested indisputably that he was in charge.

'What do they want?' Mrs Bilby frowned at them. The younger man looked around uneasily, perhaps sensing he was being observed. The older man rang the bell.

'Good afternoon.' The senior partner beamed down at Bettina as she opened the door. He brandished his clipboard ostentatiously, as though it were a badge of office. The younger man had one too.

'We aren't buying anything!' Mrs Bilby called from the front room.

'No, no, you misunderstand.' The elder's wince was a masterpiece of thinly veiled distaste. 'We are not selling anything.'

No, Bettina thought, it would have been a long time since either of these exquisite gentlemen had done any door-to-door selling; if, indeed, they ever had.

'Quite the contrary,' he continued, stepping forward. 'If we could speak to you for a few minutes, you might find it greatly to your advantage. I daresay you're far from satisfied with the state of your roof.'

'You could say that,' Bettina agreed, finding herself forced to move back as he advanced smoothly and relentlessly into the hall.

'What do they want then?' Mrs Bilby loomed in the doorway of the living room, her gaze raking them up and down; it stopped at the clipboards and she gave a dismissive sniff. 'You're never from the council!'

'Shall we say affiliated?' The younger man gave her a radiant smile.

'Say what you like.' Her disbelief was palpable; she was impervious to his charm.

'If we might sit down,' the older man suggested. 'We have something to show you that I think might interest you.'

'We're not buying anything,' Mrs Bilby reiterated, but she allowed them into the living room. 'Whoever you are.'

'Forgive me.' He dipped his hand into his pocket and brought out a small stiff square. 'My card.' He gave one to each of them.

'Huntley Forrest,' Mrs Bilby read out. 'Architect and surveyor.' She glared at him. 'We're not selling this place, either.'

'Of course not. That isn't the point at all.' Huntley Forrest sat in one of the chairs and, after a commanding glance, the younger man sank down on another.

'My colleague, Darren Ames,' he introduced him. Apparently Ames didn't rate a card of his own.

And there was something strange about the card in her hand; it didn't quite match up to the rest of the man's outfit. Surely, a man who dressed in Savile Row suits, up-to-the-minute shirts and solid gold cuff links ought to have an engraved business card and not this rather tatty square of pasteboard. It was the sort one could buy at quick-photo speed printing shops anywhere around town. Unlike everything else about Huntley Forrest – if that *was* his name – it was not designed to impress or to underline his position in life. It was simply there to convey basic information – the information he wanted one to know. Whether it was true or not was an interesting speculation.

'And you' – he consulted the papers on his clipboard briefly – 'are the Bilbys, mother and daughter.'

'Ye-es.' Mrs Bilby hated admitting it, hated even more the idea that such information was written down and in the possession of people she never knew existed. 'What have you got there?'

The inspection squad marched in from the kitchen and took up observation posts along the wall, staring at the strangers. Adolf did not appear to like what he saw, Enza was indifferent.

Pasha reflected quietly for a few moments, then edged forward cautiously, nose lifted on the scent of something meaningless to the others. Ignoring the underling, he made straight for the man in charge, sniffing at the highly polished handmade shoes.

'Handsome creature.' Huntley Forrest looked down at Pasha and leaned forward, bestowing an affable pat.

Pasha gathered himself and sprang for the man's lap, from whence he earnestly investigated the hand-stitched lapels, the crisp collar and cuffs, before settling down to scratch the side of his nose on the gold cuff links.

'Snob,' Mrs Bilby said.

'I beg your pardon?' Forrest looked startled.

'You mentioned the roof.' Bettina thought it time to bring the meeting back to its point. 'What did you have in mind?'

'Oh. Yes.' He frowned at the clipboard in one hand while the other hand absently stroked Pasha. 'My firm is engaged in some experimental work with a new company pioneering a new sort of roof covering. We've consulted with your local council and we have obtained their permission—'

Mrs Bilby's snort told him what she thought of the council. 'This is our freehold property,' she said. 'The council has nothing to do with it.'

'Of course.' He smiled charmingly. 'I was referring to planning permission, of course. It was necessary to ascertain that we wouldn't be infringing any bylaws, that sort of thing.'

'Why?' Mrs Bilby's gimlet eyes bored into him.

'Because we'd like to reroof this house as a sort of demonstration model for—'

'I've heard that one before.' Mrs Bilby looked at him with increased contempt. 'We aren't buying. We aren't contributing anything towards the cost of the materials. We aren't—'

'No, no, of course not. There's no financial obligation of any sort on your part.' The reassuring smile was fraying at the edges. 'If my colleague here could just do a quick inspection of your loft to make sure conditions are—'

'No!' Fortunately, Mrs Bilby was again in a thwarting mood, but Bettina didn't like the idea any better than she did.

The Water Board men had been anxious to get into their loft, too. Why was the loft so sought after? Could it be because lofts were where the pigeons congregated?

These men weren't the sort one usually thought of as pigeon fanciers. Diamonds, yes; pigeons, no. Carefully, she kept her hands out of her pockets, afraid of betraying something to those eyes, which, she now realized, were exceptionally watchful.

How could they know? They didn't, of course. They merely suspected. All they knew, somehow, was that the bird had last been seen in this general area.

Or was she being a little paranoid? She watched Forrest arguing half-heartedly with her mother. She saw that Ames was staring around from under lowered lids, taking in every corner of the room, his gaze returning to the two doorways leading to the rest of the house. Under the controlled exterior, he gave the impression of a man eager to be up and doing something: like searching the house. But, first, there had to be permission.

'I'm sorry you feel this way, Mrs Bilby,' Forrest said. 'We had hoped to reroof the whole terrace as a demonstration of the—'

'You're wasting your time!'

'Very well then.' Huntley Forrest made a graceful gesture of resignation. 'I'll speak to the other property owners. Perhaps when they've all agreed, you might change your mind.'

'Don't count on it!'

'No.' He looked down at his lap. 'Sorry, old boy, I'm afraid I'll have to shift you. I have the feeling we've worn out our welcome.'

There hadn't been much of a welcome to begin with, his wry smile acknowledged. He set Pasha down gently on the carpet with a final pat. Pasha moaned and tried to climb back into his lap.

'Sorry, old boy.' With a curiously awkward movement, he pushed himself up out of the chair. 'I wonder . . .' He hesitated.

Mrs Bilby's eyes narrowed, daring him to ask for something.

'I wonder if I could possibly use your telephone for a moment? It's just a local call. And I'll pay, of course,' he added hastily.

'You'd better!' Mrs Bilby glowered, unable quite to refuse such a reasonable request, especially as he had offered to pay. Bettina wondered vaguely why he didn't use his mobile phone. Perhaps he had left it at home today.

'He won't be long,' Darren Ames assured them, shifting restlessly from one foot to the other. 'We just have to check in with headquarters every so often.' He bared his teeth in that meaningless blinding smile.

Beyond him, a shadow moved at the front window beside the door, momentarily blocking out the light, as though someone had just peered in.

'What—?' Bettina started forward but, by the time she had reached the window, he was gone. Someone was turning in at Zoe's gate; he looked rather like the other man from the Water Board, although he, too, was dressed differently this afternoon.

'Thank you very much.' Huntley Forrest reappeared in the doorway, sending Darren Ames a look that brought him scurrying to his side. Pasha started forward hopefully.

'See them out, Bettina,' Mrs Bilby ordered. 'And make sure you lock the door behind them!'

'I'm terribly sorry,' Bettina murmured, following them into the hallway. 'My mother . . .'

'Yes, we understand,' Forrest said. 'Don't distress yourself. You can tell your mother' – his smile was wintery – 'I've left the payment beside the phone.'

'Oh, really, you needn't have . . .'

'*Mee-yoooorrr.*' Pasha issued a protest of his own. He didn't want this charming person to leave, but he was the only one who didn't.

'You've made quite a hit with Pasha,' Bettina said.

'It's mutual.' The man stooped to bestow a final pat. 'Perhaps another time, old boy. Goodbye.'

Bettina's eye was caught by a glint beside the telephone as she passed it and a wave of embarrassment swept over her. He had left a one-pound coin there. For a local call. She was glad she hadn't seen it while he was still here.

'Have they gone?' Mrs Bilby was beside her. 'Ah!' She saw and swooped on the pound coin. 'That's more like it.'

'It's far too much.'

'It will make up for the perfectly good pot of tea we wasted talking to them. It will be stone cold now.'

'It's still too much.'

'Speak for yourself.' Her mother glared at her. '*My* time is worth something!' She turned on her heel and marched off to the kitchen. 'I'll start a fresh kettle.'

Pasha looked from Bettina to Mrs Bilby's departing back then, wistfully, at the front door – through which all his new friends seemed to disappear. He twitched his whiskers unhappily and slumped to a mournful heap at Bettina's feet.

'Poor Pasha.' She bent to stroke him absently, her mind toying with an idea. Would it work?

She could only try. She picked up the telephone and pushed the recall button. The call was answered on the first ring.

'One-nine-eight-' – the female voice sounded oddly familiar – 'eight-nine-nine-eight.'

The number was oddly familiar, too. Bettina fished out of her pocket the scrap of paper on which Vivien had scrawled her telephone number. The numbers matched.

'Hello? Hunt? Hello?' The voice grew fearful, anxious. 'Is everything all right?'

Bettina replaced the receiver silently. She had nothing to say to Vivien Smythe. Not yet. Thoughtfully, she turned the scrap of paper over and stared down at it.

She recognized a portion of the map she had taken from Vivien's Burberry pocket that stormy day. It showed the familiar streets of the immediate area, with the blue perimeter line encircling them, but something new had been added.

Now there was a red inner line, marking the boundaries of their even more immediate neighbourhood, encircling a core of no more than five streets, with her own street in the centre.

They were narrowing the field.

Jack Rawson arrived soon after four o'clock to collect Enza. They greeted each other rapturously.

'She's been a good lass?' he asked proudly. It wasn't really a question, he had no doubt about it.

'No trouble at all,' Bettina assured him.

'She can come again,' Mrs Bilby said. 'Unlike some.' She cast a cold look at Adolf, who sneered back at her.

'Ah, he's a feisty one.' Jack Rawson regarded Adolf with a faintly proprietorial air. 'They'll be some rare kittens. Not like you, eh, poor Eunuch?'

Pasha might not understand the words, but he knew he was being mocked. He glared at Jack, then turned his back on him, crouching down in a brooding heap, closing his eyes and absenting himself from the situation, only a querulous little moan betraying that he still knew where he was and wished he wasn't.

Bettina wondered if some sixth sense was telling him how close he was to being abandoned.

'I hope they don't think they can stick us with him.' Mrs Bilby shook her head forebodingly. 'Graeme doesn't want him back without Sylvia and, if you ask me, I'd say it will be a cold day in hell before he sees Sylvia again. She made a great song and dance about meeting him in Edinburgh – and it turns out he was never in Edinburgh at all. He'd been in Brussels – and she knew it. So where has Sylvia gone, I ask you?'

'You think she's left him?' Jack Rawson's eyes gleamed. He had been on the point of leaving, now he sat down and edged his chair closer, all set for a good gossip. 'Well, it might not surprise me. I don't think his finances are as

131

steady as they used to be – and I don't think Sylvia is the kind of lady to put up with a change in her lifestyle, not if it means scrimping and saving like the rest of us.'

Bettina kept quiet, determined not to be drawn into their speculations. She was not going to betray Sylvia's confidences, although she was increasingly beginning to wonder if any of them had been true. Graeme had seemed so certain that Sylvia had known he was in Brussels.

Adolf strolled casually towards the litter box, but stopped suddenly and looked over his shoulder, as though conscious of watching eyes. Bettina looked away hastily, but he knew. He changed direction and moved towards the front hall. Was he seeking a dark and quiet corner in which to misbehave in private?

Bettina rose and, with equal casualness, followed him. The tip of his tail twitched, signalling his awareness of pursuit – and his annoyance. He reached the foot of the stairs, sat down firmly, and began washing.

Bettina leaned against the wall and regarded him sombrely. How long could this go on? ('He's the stubbornest little devil you ever saw,' May Cassidy had often said. Now he seemed determined to prove it.)

There was a burst of raucous laughter from the kitchen and Pasha scurried into the hallway, ears laid back and tail bushing. He stared around wildly with a hunted look.

'It's all right, Pasha,' Bettina soothed. 'Don't pay any attention to them. It's not your fault.'

Pasha faced her accusingly. *It's all right for you*, he seemed to say. Then something outside – a movement? a sound? – caught his attention and he moved to the front door to rear up on his hind legs and stare out of the side window.

Bettina was right behind him, alerted by his sudden tense interest. They both watched as the man at the gate stared down the path at the house, then retreated back to the edge of the pavement. He took a pair of binoculars from his pocket and trained them on the roof, turning them slowly from side to side and up and down to cover every inch of it.

Pasha gave a plaintive moan and dropped back to the floor, but Bettina continued to stare at the man. She had seen him before. He was in jeans and a Barbour jacket rather than the uniform he had originally worn, but he still had a cap on his head, although not one that was part of a chauffeur's uniform.

As she watched, he lowered the binoculars and moved on to the next house, where he thoroughly inspected Zoe's roof, and then went on again. It was obvious that he was going to check every roof in the terrace. And good luck to him; there was nothing in any of them to find.

Pasha slouched into the living room, back in his dejected mood. Adolf went after him.

And everywhere that Adolf goes ... Bettina thought grimly, trailing him.

Pasha went over to the chair Huntley Forrest had occupied and leaped up into it, nose twitching as he sniffed at the seat cushion.

Adolf decided to join him, that cushion was as comfortable as any of the others. He curled up immediately, but Pasha was restless, his nose now quivering along the divide between the cushion and the armrest.

Something in his demeanour kept Bettina watching. With growing excitement, Pasha began poking one paw down into the crack and drawing it up again.

'What are you fishing for, Pasha?' Bettina moved closer.

Pasha ignored her, intent on his goal. He probed deeper and deeper with his paw until − suddenly − he had it! Something small and gold and gleaming flew out from the upholstered crevasse and landed on the floor at Bettina's feet.

Pasha leaped out of the chair after it, but Bettina was closer. She picked it up and stared at it, oblivious to Pasha's injured claim that it was his.

It was a small gold charm: an artist's palette with two tiny brushes in the miniature thumb hole.

'Well, well, well,' Bettina said to Pasha. 'In fact, well done.'

She had the feeling that they would be seeing Vivien Smythe again before very long.

CHAPTER 13

After Jack Rawson took Enza home, Adolf retired to his carrying case to curl up and sulk. He was nearly as fed up with Bettina as she was with him.

'Good! Stay there!' She closed the door and tripped the latch. 'At least I'll know where you are.' And she would inspect the carrier when she let him out again, in case he had left something of value inside.

'You should have done that long ago,' her mother approved. 'To all of them. At last, you're showing some sense.'

'Poor Pasha, you're not very happy, are you?' Now there was time to pick him up and cuddle him. 'And you're no trouble.'

'He's brooding because he knows he's being left behind in the moonlight flit.' Mrs Bilby glared at Bettina. 'And you needn't think *we're* keeping him! Worth his weight in diamonds, indeed! He's not worth his weight in what pours out of him!'

Unlike our dear Adolf. Bettina did not say it aloud. She held Pasha a little closer and was rewarded by a soft throbbing purr of contentment. He was not to know that he had become such a problem to everyone. She buried her nose in Pasha's ruff to hide a wry smile.

'I mean it,' her mother warned. 'I'm not standing for anything else. I'll turn him in to the Cats Protection League, if I have to, but I'm not having him eating his head off around here.'

'It won't come to that,' Bettina said. 'Sylvia will be back for him. She loves him.'

'Not any more,' Mrs Bilby said. 'You heard the way Graeme was talking. Sylvia doesn't care for anything that isn't going to bring her a profit. And that goes for Graeme, too. It's only a matter of time until he admits it to himself.'

It was only too possible. But Bettina still had the feeling that Sylvia would relinquish Graeme more easily than she would let go of Pasha. At least Pasha wasn't deliberately betraying her.

But . . . was Graeme? She had only Sylvia's word for that – and Sylvia had even got the location wrong. Sylvia's word was beginning to look increasingly unreliable. Was Sylvia playing some game of her own? And, if so, what?

But Sylvia was not the only game player around. Bettina looked at her watch; it had now been some hours since Huntley Forrest had carefully planted Vivien's 'missing' charm in the depths of the armchair. It was just about time for the enigmatic Vivien to surface again with some fresh excuse for—

The telephone rang and she went to answer it. Right on cue.

'Hello . . .' She was tempted to add *Vivien*, but restrained herself. It was probably wiser not to let the mysterious Ms Smythe become aware of the fact that her game had been discovered. Especially since she wasn't quite sure what that game might be.

'Is that Miss Bilby?' Just as well she hadn't used any names. The man's voice was soft and authoritative – and not unfamiliar.

'Inspector Hughes?'

'That's right.' For a moment he sounded flattered, then his deductive processes went to work. 'Ah, the accent, I suppose.'

'Ummm . . . partly.' She felt quite, well, flustered. In truth, she had not noticed the accent at all; it was the timbre of the voice that had reached her.

'Are you feeling better?' He caught her intonation and did not seem displeased.

'Better?' For a moment, she was at a loss.

'I dropped round to your office, but you weren't there. Your boss said you'd reported in sick.'

'Oh, yes. Yes, I'm a lot better, thank you. Not well enough to go to work tomorrow, I'm afraid,' she added hastily, with a bitter thought for Adolf. 'I can't be sure. It depends on . . . how I'm feeling in the morning. These things come and go.'

'Nasty things, viruses.' He was sympathetic. 'You don't want to take any chances. Better to be safe.'

'I intend to be,' Bettina said firmly, then wavered as a new thought came to her. 'Ummm . . . why did you call at the office?'

'Just a few more questions,' he said smoothly. 'Perhaps I might come round now, if it's convenient? It won't take long.'

'Yes, I suppose so.' Somehow, this didn't sound very official. She thought the police just turned up at the door without worrying about anyone's convenience. That was what they had done before.

'BETTINA!' Her mother's voice was loud enough to be heard at the other end of the line. 'Get out here! That Adolf is going to be sick. Get him out of the house!'

'Yes, I'm coming.' She turned back to the receiver. 'I'm sorry—'

'I heard,' he said. 'Go ahead. I'll be round shortly.'

Adolf was threshing about in his carrying case, hunched up and heaving, making distressing sounds and bumping into the sides of the case as he struggled.

'Get him out of here, cage and all! Pick it up and take it out into the garden and dump him. He's having a fit!'

'It's probably a hairball.' And, with any luck, Adolf would cough it up with the diamond neatly in the middle of it, like a pearl in an oyster. Or perhaps it was just the diamond itself.

'I don't care what it is – get him out of here!'

'Easy, Adolf, easy.' Bettina bent and opened the door of the case. 'Come on, now.'

Adolf backed out of the case, still heaving and retching.

He backed halfway across the kitchen floor before seeming to realize that he was out and free.

'Come on, Adolf,' Bettina encouraged. 'Cough it up. Spit it out. You'll feel a lot better.'

Adolf stepped back, then remained very still and hunched over, mouth open. His head bobbed convulsively a few times then, abruptly, he straightened up and shook himself.

'All right, Adolf?' Bettina watched him with concern. 'Are you all right now?'

Adolf sat down, swallowed hard twice, and regarded her with bright-eyed interest.

False alarm.

'I still say put him out!' Mrs Bilby glared at Adolf. 'He'll only sneak around to some dark corner and sick it up there.'

'I'll watch him,' Bettina promised. 'Very carefully.'

'You should have better things to do.' Her mother sniffed. 'Wasting all your time and energy on ruddy cats.'

When she should be wasting it on a ruddy mother. Bettina could easily identify the underlying cause for complaint.

Pasha had been watching Adolf's performance with great interest; now he strolled over to touch noses with him. There appeared to be an exchange of thought, then they both turned and stared at Bettina meaningfully.

'I suppose a bit of cod-liver oil might soothe your throat,' she agreed. 'And Pasha could always use a little more.'

'I can't sit here and watch you spoiling those cats!' Mrs Bilby got to her feet. 'I'm going to watch television. Call me when dinner's ready.'

Both cats seemed more relaxed with Mrs Bilby out of the way. They tucked into their cod-liver oil with gusto.

Bettina wished that she could feel more relaxed. She surveyed Adolf anxiously. Had that coughing fit meant that the diamond was caught somewhere well above the point it could reasonably be expected to have reached by now? If so, did that mean Adolf could retain it longer?

138

She tried to tell herself that twenty-four hours wasn't all that long, but she wasn't very convinced. It seemed like forever. Still, Adolf was showing no ill effects – unless that retching had been the start of complications. She wished she knew more about feline anatomy. Perhaps she ought to ring Zoe at the library and ask her to bring home some books about—

The doorbell rang, startling her.

'BET—'

'I heard it! I'm coming!'

'Well, you needn't snap my head off!' Her mother's voice was aggrieved. 'I'm only trying to help.'

A daughter's place is in the wrong. She'd been stuck in this house all day, when she might have had the respite of being at work. And that after being stuck in the house all Bank Holiday weekend. Worse, she was trapped for the unforeseeable future – all her plans dependent on Adolf's digestive system. No wonder her nerves were twanging and her temper shortening.

'Oh! Inspector Hughes!' Preoccupied by her thoughts, she had forgotten about him. 'That was quick. I wasn't expecting you so soon.'

'I was nearby when I rang.' His smile was so guileless, it aroused a faint suspicion. He seemed to be alone.

'Come in.' She stepped back and looked beyond him. 'No constable today?'

'His shift ended. He's got a home to go to.'

'And you haven't?'

'Not up here. Not much of a one in Sussex, either, since my wife died. I brought Timmy up with me. That helps.'

'BETTINA! Are you going to stand out in the hall all night? Who's out there with you?'

'It's Inspector Hughes, Mother.' With an apologetic shrug, she led him into the living room. 'He has a few more questions for us.'

'Humph!' Mrs Bilby eyed him coldly. 'I thought policemen were supposed to get it right the first time. Or does that only apply when they're lifting valuables?'

139

'Mother!' Bettina turned to Inspector Hughes. 'I'm so sorry—'

'Quite all right.' He cut off her apology. 'I take it whence it comes.'

'Humph!'

'The fact is, madam' – he faced Mrs Bilby sternly – 'most inquiries are preliminary. As we learn more, the situation clarifies and we know the additional questions we need to ask in order to get at the truth of the matter.'

'*Humph!*' Mrs Bilby picked up the remote control and began channel hopping just to show how unimpressed she was.

'Our proceedings are governed,' he continued smoothly, 'by the information we discover or, in this case, don't discover.'

Mrs Bilby was still pretending obliviousness, but she hesitated, allowing the screen to fill with the image of a rock star being interviewed, any word of whose language would ordinarily have had her switching channels instantly.

Bettina, watchful as any of the cats, waited her moment to dart in and gain possession of the remote control.

'I would like to speak to you' – he raised his voice over the blare – 'regarding this matter.'

Mrs Bilby stared at the television screen, her thumb moved imperceptibly and the sound volume increased.

'With your permission . . . ?' Inspector Hughes barely waited for Bettina's nod before crossing the room in a few swift strides, bending and switching the electricity off at the plug.

'Oh!' Mrs Bilby gasped with outrage as the screen went dark. 'You put that back on immediately!'

'After just a few questions, madam.' Inspector Hughes smiled unpleasantly. 'Unless you'd care to accompany me to the station house and answer them there?'

'What? And have all the neighbours see me being driven away in a police car?'

'The choice is yours, madam.' Inspector Hughes waited.

Adolf and Pasha strolled in to see what was going on.

'Blasted cats!' Mrs Bilby glared from them to Bettina, as though trying to decide which to blame for her predicament. 'It's police harassment, that's what it is.'

'Doubtless the cats will act as witnesses, if you care to register an official complaint, madam.'

Adolf yawned hugely and settled down to await developments.

'There aren't so many of them today,' Inspector Hughes noted in an aside to Bettina while Mrs Bilby composed herself.

'Two of them have gone home,' Bettina said. 'Adolf's owner won't be back until next week and Pasha . . .' What could one say about Pasha? 'Pasha will be here for a while yet.'

'You're not keeping him!' Mrs Bilby snapped. 'Don't you dare let yourself think that for one minute!' She glared from Bettina to Inspector Hughes as she spoke. She wasn't going to allow Bettina to keep *him*, either – just in case she was getting any ideas.

'What did you want to ask?' Bettina quickly tried to avert Hughes's attention from her mother's clear but unspoken message.

'We've told you everything we know! There can't be any questions left. It's just some kind of excuse.' For what, Mrs Bilby fortunately did not specify.

'You told us the workmen were from the Water Board,' Inspector Hughes said. 'How did you know that?'

'Well, it was obvious, wasn't it? Who else would be splashing around in puddles in the pouring rain?'

'Then you didn't see any identification?'

'Why, no,' Bettina said slowly, remembering. 'We just assumed . . . or possibly from the council . . .'

'Why?' Mrs Bilby butted in sharply. 'Who were they? Where did they come from?'

'They weren't from the Water Board,' Inspector Hughes said. 'And they weren't from the council. Both authorities deny having had any people in this area at all. There were no priority problems here, the flooding was much worse in other sections of town. They had to concentrate on those.'

'I *told* you to ask for their credentials!' Mrs Bilby trumpeted, glaring at Bettina. 'Burglars, I knew it!'

'Burglars are unlikely in this neighbourhood,' Hughes said dismissively. 'At least, that sort of burglar. Amateurs, chancers, yes. But not planners.'

'Then who were they?' Mrs Bilby challenged. 'We'd never seen any of them before. The whole place was swarming with strange men unblocking drains. You can't tell me they were just public-spirited citizens!'

'I wouldn't even try,' Inspector Hughes assured her. 'We're working hard on finding out who they were. You wouldn't have any ideas?' Over Mrs Bilby's head, he looked at Bettina.

'As Mother said, we'd never seen any of them before.' She hoped that he wouldn't think to ask if she'd seen any of them since.

And yet . . . she was growing very tired of trying to keep everything to herself. Inspector Hughes seemed so very sympathetic . . . could he be trusted? He had nothing to do with the corruption that had tainted the local force; he had been brought in specially from another part of the country to help. Perhaps she could confide in him . . . perhaps he could help her . . .

'Why ask us?' Mrs Bilby snapped. 'It's up to you to find out who they are. That's *your* job!'

No, she couldn't talk in front of her mother. And, unable to leave the house, trapped by Adolf, she couldn't arrange to meet Inspector Hughes somewhere else to tell him the story. The best she could manage would be to follow him to the front door when he left, step outside with him and try to speak rapidly before her mother became restive and began shouting for her or, worse, came out after her to see what she was doing.

'If we could go back to the beginning,' Inspector Hughes said patiently; suddenly there was a notebook and pen in

142

his hands. 'Don't try to look for something you think might be significant, or anything you think I might want to hear. Just start at the beginning and tell me all about your encounter with these men. When you first noticed them, what they were doing, when they came to speak to you, everything they said . . .'

It was half an hour later when they had run out of details and Inspector Hughes closed his notebook. The fragrance of a well-cooked meal, ready to be eaten, was permeating the living room. The cats were moving restively, starting towards the kitchen and looking back over their shoulders, wondering why no one else was moving.

'I think that's all, thank you,' Inspector Hughes said reluctantly, looking a bit wistful.

'I should hope so!' Mrs Bilby said. 'Now maybe you can get on with your work and leave us in peace.'

'Gladly, madam.' He no longer looked so wistful; the tastiest meal in the world would turn to ashes in the wrong company. 'If you think of anything you've forgotten, please ring me at the station.'

'Don't hold your breath!'

'I wouldn't dream of it, madam.' He was in the front hall before the last word was out and advancing on the front door.

'I'm sorry.' Bettina was right behind him. 'Mother is just—' She moved in front of him and opened the door, ready to step out.

'Stop apologizing!' he said roughly. 'She's not your fault.'

'No, but I—' A movement at her feet caught her attention; she looked down. 'Oh, Bluebell – what are you doing out at this hour?'

Bluebell crossed the threshold into the light of the hall-way, stopped and looked up at Bettina unhappily, uttering a piteous little mew.

'What's the matter, Bluebell?' Bettina stooped to her.

143

'Isn't Zoe home yet? She'll be back soon. It must be her late night.'

But that didn't explain what Bluebell was doing out so late; both of the Romes always took good care to see that Bluebell was safely inside before night fell and marauding toms began prowling.

Bluebell mewed again and moved a bit farther into the hallway before stopping again and, mewling complaints, shook one paw after another. She hated getting her feet wet.

And her paws were wet . . . and red.

'Here, girl.' Inspector Hughes crouched and spoke soothingly. 'Come here, let's have a look at you.'

Adolf and Pasha materialized at her side, sniffing at her paws with mouths open and tongues curled back, seeming intrigued yet revolted at the message coming through to them.

Bluebell shied back, frightened and further upset at all this sudden attention. She skirted round the humans and moved down the hallway in search of the comfort of the kitchen with its warm familiar smell of cooking.

'She isn't limping.' Hughes started after her. Adolf and Pasha fell in on either side, escorting her.

'Here, Bluebell . . .' Bettina swooped on the cat, capturing her. 'Let me see. Shh, it's all right, darling. Let me see.'

'Hold her,' Hughes directed, closing in and taking a forepaw gently. 'Shh, it's all right, girl, it's all right. Just let us take a look.'

Bluebell wriggled uneasily, but did not try to scratch as Hughes inspected her paw. He parted the fur and they could see that the blood dyed only the outer hairs. Closer to the skin, the fur was soft and pale and unmarked. Hughes checked each paw in turn and nodded. He stroked Bluebell's head lightly and looked at Bettina.

'She isn't hurt,' he said, 'but I'm afraid someone is. She's been treading in it.'

'Zoe!' Bettina gasped.

'Do you have a key?' Hughes was wise in the ways of friendly neighbours.

'BETTINA! Is that policeman still here? What are you doing out there?'

'Through the kitchen,' Bettina directed quickly. 'They never lock the back door. It will be faster.' She looked down at Bluebell irresolutely.

'Bring the cat with you,' he said, already at the kitchen door. 'We don't want to start *her* off again.'

'BETTINA! Where are you? Answer me!'

'Just popping round to Zoe,' Bettina called. 'I'll be right back.' She glanced down and, with a cold chill, saw that a smudge of blood had transferred from Bluebell's paw to her blouse.

Zoe . . . She shuddered and stopped short just outside the door, suddenly unable to move.

'Doing fine,' Hughes murmured encouragingly, closing the door behind them.

She should have put the back-door light on; it was awfully dark out here. That was why she couldn't move. It was too dark and she couldn't see a thing.

'Which way?' Hughes took her elbow, his hand was steadying.

'Through here.' She led him through the gap in the hedge. Bluebell began to wriggle as they approached Zoe's back door; she didn't want to go in.

Neither did Bettina. She had to brace herself, clutching Bluebell tighter, to step across the threshold.

The light was on in the kitchen. Bettina looked at it. It seemed quite dim. Either Zoe needed a new bulb, or there was another power reduction on.

She looked at the table, where a cup of tea had overturned and spilled across the table, dripping to the floor to merge with . . .

She looked at the undrawn curtains framing the window, at the stove, at the closed door leading to the larder.

She looked anywhere to keep from looking at the battered and bloodstained body sprawled on the floor beside the table.

CHAPTER 14

'Stay there,' Hughes said. 'Don't move. Don't touch anything.' He crossed to the still form and knelt beside it, reaching for Mrs Rome's wrist, searching for a pulse.

Bettina looked at the window again. At the darkness outside, blotting out the garden, at the bottom of which another body had been found. She looked away. There was no comfort, no escape, in looking out of the window.

'Where's the telephone?' Inspector Hughes straightened up, frowning.

'Is she . . . ?'

'Still a flicker, I think. We need the ambulance – fast. The telephone?'

'In the living room.' She started forward, but he waved her back.

'I'll do it.' His grim tone promised that he could get faster service than she could – and that there were other calls he had to make. 'Can you get something to cover her with?'

'A blanket . . . upstairs . . .' This time he let her move out to the staircase. She noted vaguely that he had just countermanded his own order not to touch anything – but, of course, saving a life had to take precedence over preserving evidence.

Bluebell quietened as she carried her into Zoe's room and set her down on the carpet while she took a blanket from the oak linen chest. She was about to carry it downstairs, leaving Bluebell behind, when she saw that the cat, with an air of fastidious distaste, had lifted one paw to her mouth to begin to wash it.

'No! Don't *do* that!' She dropped the blanket and caught up Bluebell, rushing her to the bathroom, where she held each paw under the running tap until the worst of the blood had disappeared down the drain and the water ran clear, leaving only a faint pink tinge to Bluebell's fur. Then she dabbed at the paws with a towel and dropped Bluebell back in Zoe's room, picked up the blanket, shut the door and hurried down the stairs.

She felt a crushing sense of guilt, although the whole process could only have taken a minute or two. Surely nothing dire – nothing worse – could have happened to Mrs Rome in that time. And she couldn't – she *couldn't* – have let Bluebell lick that blood from her paws. Perhaps that might count as destroying evidence, but she couldn't help it. She could not have let Zoe come home and find her mother's blood on Bluebell.

She was prepared to argue her case, but Inspector Hughes made no comment on the length of her absence, perhaps it hadn't taken so long, after all. Hughes took the blanket from her and draped it over the still form, leaving the face uncovered, she was relieved to see.

'They'll be here soon,' he said. 'Why don't you sit down?' Already there was a faint shriek of sirens in the far distance, coming closer.

'Zoe,' Bettina said. 'Someone will have to tell Zoe.' She waited, hoping he would say that that would be done by a policewoman when one arrived. They were trained for situations like this, weren't they?

'Yes.' Instead, he nodded agreement, his nod aimed vaguely in the direction of the telephone. 'She can meet us at the hospital. It will save time and keep her out of the way here while the crime team gets to work.'

'Crime . . . ?' She hadn't thought of it like that, she hadn't really been thinking at all. Every mental process had seemed to stop when she realized Bluebell had blood on her paws.

'Bluebell . . .' Her mind caught at an acceptable, a normal, activity. 'I'd better take Bluebell home with me.

There'll be strangers tramping through the house, frightening her, leaving doors open . . .'

The siren was deafening now, underlining her fears, then it stopped suddenly. Outside.

'Take the cat away now,' Hughes said, 'and telephone from your house. It's going to be hectic here.'

The doorbell pealed urgently, proving his point. Bettina accompanied him into the front hall and started up the stairs as he opened the door. Suddenly, she wanted nothing more than to get out of that house, even at the price of having to telephone Zoe with the horrible news of what had happened.

Zoe kept Bluebell's carrying case in her closet; Bettina took it out. Bluebell had been curled up asleep on the bed and muttered a drowsy protest as Bettina bundled her into the case and carried her out into the hall.

The hallway and stairs were being sporadically transformed into an eerie blue cavern by the flashing lights on the vehicles outside.

Two paramedics were carrying Mrs Rome on a stretcher through the lower hallway. Bettina waited on the stairs to allow them a clear passage. As they went past, Mrs Rome stirred faintly, her lips barely moved.

'. . . don't . . . know . . . don't . . .' It was less than a whisper, just a faint suggestion of words. '. . . don't . . . know . . .'

The door opened and they carried her through to the waiting ambulance.

Outside, a crowd was gathering like vultures, drawn by the sirens and lights. Bettina recognized Jack Rawson and Graeme Martin among the faces. Others were less familiar, from streets farther afield.

At the very edge of the gathering, her face distorted by some emotion and unearthly in the blue illumination, there was — wasn't there? — yet another well-known face.

Bettina blinked and looked again, but the face was gone. Had she really seen it at all? Or had Vivien Smythe arrived in pursuit of her own ends and chosen to disappear again,

149

horrified by all the attention suddenly surrounding her quarry?

The rest of the crowd consolidated, huddling together, talking among themselves, watching avidly . . . waiting for some victim they could accost for details.

Bettina fled through the kitchen. Men in uniform were clustered around the table and the blood-splattered floor beneath it. One or two looked up at her sharply as she opened the back door.

'It's all right,' Inspector Hughes told them and they lost interest.

Which was more than could be said for her mother. Although Mrs Bilby had been stationed behind the living room curtains, the sound of the back door opening rang like a clap of thunder in her ears and she was in the kitchen before Bettina had closed the door behind her.

'What's going on?' Mrs Bilby demanded. 'What's happened over there?'

'I have to ring Zoe.' Bettina deposited the carrying case in its accustomed place and headed for the telephone with her mother following.

Bettina spoke briefly to Zoe against a background of gasps, shrieks and mutterings from Mrs Bilby. When she rang off, her mother gasped dramatically and reeled back against the wall, hand to her heart.

'Burglars! I told you so!' Mrs Bilby hyperventilated for a few moments before continuing.

Bettina occupied the respite in ringing for a taxi to take her to the hospital to meet Zoe.

'You're never going to leave me here alone!' Mrs Bilby protested. 'Tonight? When who knows what monster is prowling about outside!'

'The police are all over the place,' Bettina pointed out. 'They'll be here for hours yet. You'll be perfectly safe. Where's Adolf?'

'That cat again!' Mrs Bilby brought her other hand up to her heart and clutched at her bodice frantically. 'You're worried about a wretched cat when your own mother—'

150

'You'll be all right.' Bettina could not quite control her impatience. 'Adolf?' She raised her voice. 'Adolf?'

'Poor Dora Rome beaten up and nearly dead – and you worrying about a bloody cat! Poor Dora, she should have been over here, then she'd never have known her house was being broken into until it was all done and the burglar well away . . .' Mrs Bilby's eyes widened suddenly, her face sagged, a new and horrifying thought struck her.

'*She* might have been here – but *I* might have been over *there*! He might have broken in to find the two of us together having tea. He might have tried to kill me, too!' She was hyperventilating in earnest now.

'*I* might be in that ambulance with Dora. He might have killed *me!*' Her hands clawed at her bosom. 'Oh, my heart! Where are my pills?'

'In your pocket,' Bettina said. That had been decided and arranged long ago. It was the closest and safest place for them, easily reached and always to hand.

'Oh, there you are, Adolf.' He had come out from under the sofa. Automatically, she bent to check; it was clean and clear under there.

Adolf sat down and gave her a huffy look. He was a clean cat and she ought to have more faith in him.

'Sorry, Adolf, but it's back in your cage.' She caught him up and carried him into the kitchen. 'I've got to go out.'

'And leave me here alone!' Her mother was not going to forgive this defection easily.

'Why don't you ask Jack Rawson to come in and sit with you for a while?' She turfed Adolf into his case. Later, she would take a good look round the house to make sure he hadn't relieved himself in some dark corner while she was next door with Inspector Hughes.

'*Sit* with me? Like a baby-sitter? Or' – her mother sneered – 'a cat-sitter? And you can lock up that Pasha, too, while you're at it,' she added. 'I'm not having him roaming through the house, either.'

151

The telephone rang; an unfamiliar voice reported that her taxi was waiting outside.

'I'll have a word with Jack Rawson as I go past,' she told her mother. 'He's in the crowd outside.'

'You haven't had your dinner.' Her mother made a last-ditch attempt to stop her.

'I'm not hungry. Give it to Mr Rawson. And don't wait up for me.'

'I'm not going to cry,' Zoe said. 'Not yet. She's still hanging on. They don't think there's much hope, but they're not giving up on her. Neither am I.'

Bettina nodded; she couldn't offer any hope, either. Zoe had not seen her mother at her worst. Mrs Rome was so small and frail, it was unthinkable that anyone could have used violence against her.

'They've got a policewoman sitting with her,' Zoe said. 'To take down anything she says if she recovers consciousness.' She shook her head. 'It all seems so unreal, so impossible. They don't even know when it happened.'

'Mother and I were home all day,' Bettina said, feeling the same disbelief. 'We didn't hear a thing – and the walls aren't that thick. I don't know when it might have happened.' That was something else unthinkable: how long had Mrs Rome been lying there on the cold linoleum?

'No one knows.' Zoe's mouth twitched briefly in a sardonic smile. 'The police – some of them – seem quite annoyed that she wasn't dead. Then rigor mortis would have set in and they'd have had a better chance of pinpointing when it happened. It's just as well I was on the desk all afternoon from two o'clock onwards, in full view of the public.'

'They wouldn't suspect you.' Bettina was shocked.

'Why not?' Zoe shrugged. 'Most murders are domestic. That usually means the spouse did it. The fact is, you're not really safe from anyone in the family.'

'The neighbourhood was full of strangers all day. The police ought to be trying to find them.'

'But why?' Zoe frowned. 'I don't understand. We've always been such a quiet, peaceful neighbourhood. Dull as ditchwater, in fact. What's going on?'

This was neither the time nor the place to try to explain. Bettina felt a sharp pang of guilt. She should have done something earlier, told Inspector Hughes as soon as he first appeared on the scene. Now he would have to be told and it would be even more awkward because the clear implication was that she had trusted him no more than her mother had. While her mother had been consistently and overtly insulting, her own behaviour would be the more hurtful because they had seemed to get along so well, with an underlying . . . what . . . ?

And she must tell Zoe, too. More guilt. If she had told Zoe earlier, could they have done something to prevent what had happened?

'Still here?' A friendly nurse smiled at Zoe. 'You might as well go home and get some rest, you know. There's nothing you can do here. If there's any change in Mrs Rome's condition, we'll call you at once.'

Bettina and Zoe exchanged glances. Neither of them liked that 'at once' with its intimation of a wild dash back to the bedside for a last goodbye. The clear implication was that any change was going to be for the worse.

It was all her fault. Rather, the fault of those diamonds. Again she felt that burning sensation in her pocket. And what was Adolf doing right now? Or not doing? She had to get home to see, but she could not leave Zoe here alone. Nor could she let Zoe return to her own house, to the devastation of walking into that kitchen and seeing the story of what had happened spilled out in her mother's blood across the floor.

'Come back with me,' she said. 'You can stay in the guest room tonight. Bluebell is already with us.' They could face the horror better in the morning. If she could get up before Zoe, she could do something about cleaning up the kitchen—

'I think it would be better if she came back to *my* guest

153

room.' A male voice spoke unexpectedly behind them.

'William!' Zoe gasped. They whirled to face him.

'What on earth are you doing here?' Bettina asked. A sudden suspicion rustled at the back of her mind, as ridiculous as suspecting Zoe, but . . . 'How did you know . . . ?'

'Your mother telephoned me.' He spoke as stiffly as if he had just read her mind. 'Quite properly.'

'I see.' Bettina saw that her mother had been interfering again, matchmaking Zoe and William, throwing them together at a time when Zoe could use someone to cling to. And, incidentally, removing William as a possible threat to the comfort of Mrs Bilby's own settled life. Bettina felt a sense of impending loss. Not that she wanted William for herself, but it had been rather comforting to think that there was someone she could fall back on. And surely William deserved more than that. So did she.

'Oh, I don't know,' Zoe said miserably. 'I just don't know.' She looked at Bettina, halfway between hysterical laughter and tears. The old joke stood between them, only it wasn't so funny now. It wasn't funny at all.

'Go ahead,' Bettina said. 'Everything will look better in the morning.'

Including William? Zoe's quirked eyebrow conveyed briefly, with a flicker of her old mockery. Then he took her arm and she leaned towards him gratefully, all mockery gone.

'She'll be at this number,' William said masterfully, handing the nurse his card. 'Please let us know as soon as you have any news.'

'We'll do that.' The nurse took his card. 'Don't worry – and try to get some sleep,' she said to Zoe. 'Have you anything to take?'

'I'll give her something,' William said. 'I don't use them often, but I do have some sleeping pills.'

'That's fine,' the nurse approved, turning away, moving on to the next task, already forgetting about them – until there was some news to report.

'Let's go.' William tugged gently at Zoe's arm. He looked

over her head at Bettina. 'We'll drop you back at the house.'

'Thank you,' she said. It was already '*We*', the beginning of the newer, stronger alliance. She looked at Zoe, who did not meet her eye. 'Do you want to pick up Bluebell?'

'She'll be all right there,' William said.

'I'll be round first thing in the morning,' Zoe said.

'Perhaps second or third thing,' William amended softly. 'Those pills are strong enough to keep her knocked out for a while.'

CHAPTER 15

Despite wishing that she had been able to ask William for
a couple of his sleeping pills, Bettina fell into an exhausted
slumber almost as soon as her head hit the pillow. If there
were strange motor cars patrolling through the night, she
didn't hear them. It was just past ten when she awoke in
the morning.

The cats were still in their carriers when she entered
the kitchen. Restless and complaining, they let her know
just how badly they were being treated. They hadn't even
been fed.

'Mother?' Suddenly frightened, she rushed back upstairs. 'Mother?' Her mother's bedroom was empty, the
bedcovers turned back for airing.

Bettina returned to the kitchen, checking all the other
rooms on the way. Mrs Bilby was not in the house.

'All right.' She let Bluebell and Pasha out of their pens,
but not Adolf, and opened the back door, allowing them
out into the garden. They swept past her like a tidal wave,
only one need more urgent than breakfast.

Adolf howled and stamped about in his cage. It was
unfair, it was unjust, he was being kept prisoner – and he
was innocent.

'All right, Adolf.' Bettina let him out, but shook her
head as he dashed over to the back door. 'No, not you.
You stay in here.'

Adolf had another temper tantrum, but it did him no
good. At last, he capitulated, stalking stiff-legged to the
litter box, outrage in every fibre of his being. Glaring at
Bettina, he squatted, but only liquid was released.

'You're not cooperating,' Bettina said reproachfully. 'Never mind, at least you'll get your breakfast first.' She filled his bowl and, when he was fully occupied, opened the door to see if the others were ready to come in.

Pasha was waiting at the door, but Bluebell was nowhere in sight. Probably trying her luck at her own back door, Bettina decided. Life would be so much easier if one could only explain it to cats.

'Bluebell . . .' she called. 'Over here, Bluebell. Breakfast . . .'

Pasha was already in the kitchen, gazing with dissatisfaction at his empty bowl. Nothing was the way it should be these days.

'Sorry, Pasha.' Bettina closed the door, nipping in the bud Adolf's dash for freedom, and poured Pasha's breakfast into his bowl.

Pasha, a gentleman, meowed his thanks. It was probably just as well she could not interpret Adolf's snarled remark, it sounded vile.

Bettina was just sitting down to her tea and toast when the back door opened and Mrs Bilby came in, Bluebell at her heels.

'Mother, are you all right?' Bettina leaped up and quickly poured another cup of tea. Her mother looked terrible, white-faced and trembling. 'Sit down. Where have you been?'

'Next door, of course.' Mrs Bilby slumped into the chair, staring into space, only her voice seemed to have any strength. 'Cleaning up. I couldn't leave that for Zoe to face. It was my duty. The least' – her voice broke – 'I could do for poor Dora.'

Bluebell wound around her ankles, chirruping anxiously.

'Oh, Mother!' Bettina put milk and extra sugar in the tea and pushed over her own buttered toast. 'You should have waited. I was going to do that.'

'Dora was my friend, long before you were born,' Mrs Bilby said. 'It was up to me to do it.'

'Drink your tea.' Bettina moved away to put more bread in the toaster and fill Bluebell's dish. 'And stop using the past tense. Mrs Rome isn't dead yet.'

'And do you think she's going to survive?'

Bettina could not answer.

'No.' Mrs Bilby shook her head and reached automatically for her cup. 'We weren't to know it the other night, but when poor Dora turned up the ace of spades, she was turning it up for herself.'

Adolf finished his breakfast and stalked over to the back door with a determined gleam in his eye. He sat down beside it, staring up at the knob. When this brought no result, he emitted a long, loud howl, making his wishes clear.

'Oh, let him out,' Mrs Bilby said. 'What does it matter?'

She could not tell her mother how much it mattered.

'Why don't you lie down for a while?' she suggested instead. 'You're looking . . . very tired.' On closer inspection, her mother's appearance frightened her. Mrs Bilby looked more than tired; she looked exhausted . . . and old. Much older suddenly than her actual years, drained of all energy and at the end of her tether.

'I can't help remembering,' Mrs Bilby said, 'the way Dora's Joe and my Arthur died together on that fishing trip. Now Dora's almost gone and I feel terrible. Maybe it was meant for us to go together, too.'

'Don't talk like that!' Bettina hadn't intended to speak so sharply, but her nerves were on edge. A shudder ran through her. 'It's like tempt—'

'Tempting fate? Or acknowledging it?' Mrs Bilby stared into space unseeingly. 'I've never admitted it before but, ever since Joe and Arthur went like that, I've thought it often. It's as though all our destinies have been entwined since we first moved into these houses. Perhaps you and Zoe will die together, too.'

'Highly unlikely.' Bettina fought for control; one of them on the verge of hysteria was enough.

'Oh, I don't know. All it would take would be an accident in that car of hers – you know she drives too fast – and that would be it! Two families wiped out completely.' She nodded reflectively. 'I suppose your cousin Anselm would get the house.'

'You'll feel better after you've rested,' Bettina said firmly.

Mrs Bilby snorted.

'If you don't want to go up to your room, you can lie down on the sofa.' At this point, her mother looked as though the stairs would be too much for her.

'I've no time to lie down,' Mrs Bilby said. 'I want to get over to the hospital and visit Dora.'

'I'm not sure they'll let you in.' Bettina tried to dissuade her. 'And Mrs Rome won't be able to speak to you, she's unconscious.'

'Just the same, I'll be there.' Mrs Bilby pushed herself away from the table and rose heavily to her feet, panting slightly from that much exertion.

'Let me call Zoe first and see if she's heard anything.' Bettina's concern grew. Her mother was already dangerously upset. If she got there and found that Dora Rome had died during the night, the shock might be too much for her.

But no one answered the telephone at William's house, although she let it ring for an inordinate length of time. That could mean that Zoe and William had gone to work ... or that they were on their way over here ... or that the dreaded summons had arrived and they were at the hospital.

'No answer?' Mrs Bilby watched her bleakly. 'Never mind her then. Just get me a taxi.'

'In a minute.' Bettina rang the hospital first, to hear that there had been no change in Mrs Rome's condition. She looked from her mother to Adolf irresolutely. 'Would you like me to come with you?'

'And leave your precious cats?' Mrs Bilby jeered, with

a faint return of her old spirit. 'I can manage on my own, thank you. Just order me that taxi.'

The weather was running true to form. Having stormed and raged all over the Bank Holiday weekend, it now provided a perfect early autumn day, warm and sunny, for everyone to sit in their offices and look out on.

Bluebell and Pasha, remembering that they had been allowed out in the garden earlier in the day, were now agitating to go out again. Adolf hadn't given up hope, his voice was loudest of all.

'Not right now,' Bettina said firmly, glad that her mother wasn't there to complain about the noise.

Adolf realized the truth of the situation well ahead of the others. With a disgusted look at Bettina, he leaped for the counter and sat down to stare out of the window in a put-upon manner. Then he snapped to alert attention and moved up against the pane, staring intently towards the end of the garden.

Bettina could not resist the pull of curiosity. What was Adolf witnessing this time? She leaned over him, her gaze following his.

The bushes were rustling, branches waving about wildly – and yet there was no wind. As she watched, a man emerged from the thick of the bushes and crouched there.

For a moment, she thought it was the bogus Water Board workman again, then he straightened up and half turned, becoming identifiable: Graeme Martin. What was he doing prowling about their garden, acting as though he were looking for something . . . or someone?

Surely, he didn't expect to find Sylvia under the bushes. Or did he? Had he learned something to make him suspect that Sylvia had never reached Edinburgh, that she had not gone far from the house? That she had, perhaps, been the first to encounter whatever murderous maniac had been prowling the neighbourhood.

Graeme suddenly looked directly at the house. Instinctively, Bettina stepped back before reminding herself sharply that she was not her mother, to hide behind curtains – and also that it was *her* garden and it was for Graeme to explain himself for trespassing.

He waved and started towards the back door, the same thought perhaps occurring to him.

Bettina gestured to him to wait a minute while she shooed the cats away from the door. He occupied the time in trying to smooth his dishevelled hair back into place and brush the twigs and leaves from his suit.

'Good morning, Bettina.' He slipped through the door as she opened it slightly, still fending off Adolf. 'Everything all right here?'

'What's the matter? Why were you—?'

'I thought I heard a cat crying.' A safe excuse in this district. He took a swift look around. 'They seem to be all present and accounted for. Hello, Pasha, how are you today?'

Pasha looked at him and beyond him; no one else there. Pasha turned and stalked away, his tail shot up suddenly and the end twitched in unmistakable insult.

'I'll grant you he's Sylvia's cat,' Graeme said in an injured tone, 'but does he have to be so bloody rude to everyone else? I'm the one who pays for his cat food, after all. And his damned cod-liver oil.'

Since she had never heard Graeme utter a comment about Pasha that wasn't bloody rude, it was hardly surprising that Pasha returned his sentiments, Bettina thought.

'Bettina, what's going on around here?' Dismissing Pasha, Graeme turned to her. 'What happened to Mrs Rome? I saw the ambulance last night. And the police. Was it a heart attack? How is she?'

'They're not sure she's going to survive. It wasn't a heart attack. An intruder broke in and beat her almost to death—' Bettina stopped. *Broke in.* One said it so automatically – and it wasn't true. There had been no signs of a break-in at either back door or front.

'Here? On our street? That's terrible!' Graeme looked stunned. 'And Sylvia and I moved here because we

161

thought this would be a good place to live, much safer than in the city. Perhaps we'll have to think again.'

Of course, the back door was never locked. Bettina was still thinking. But no intruder, no stranger, would know that. Was it possible that Mrs Rome had known the person who had entered her house and then treated her so savagely? *'Don't know . . .'* she had kept repeating as the paramedics carried her away. Did that mean, not that she didn't know her attacker, but didn't know the information he had been trying to beat out of her?

'Bettina? Bettina? Are you all right?' Graeme was watching her with concern. 'Is something wrong? What is it?'

'I just thought—' No, Graeme was not a person to confide in. 'I thought I heard something,' she finished as the doorbell rang. 'Excuse me, that may be Zoe.'

'Poor Zoe.' Graeme was behind her as she entered the front hall. 'Is there anything I can do?'

'Catch Adolf.' She nearly tripped over the black and white blur streaking past her. 'Don't let him get out when I open the door.'

'Oh. Right.' He bent and scooped up Adolf, who objected violently. 'Ow! You little—' They retreated down the hallway, swearing at each other.

Bettina opened the door cautiously, in case Adolf escaped, and gazed appreciatively at narrow tartan trousers tucked into dark green, butter-soft leather boots. The gilt chain of the matching shoulder bag gleamed in the deep fuzz of a long, dark green, mohair jacket. Bettina wondered if they still called the colour forest green – and if there were some subliminal message in that. Or a private joke.

'May I come in?' Vivien Smythe asked brightly.

Still bemused, Bettina stepped back to allow the world's best-dressed market researcher to enter.

'Thanks awfully.' Vivien blinked, stepping into the gloom of the hallway from the bright sunshine outside and moved directly into the living room. 'I'm terribly sorry to disturb you again, but I've been racking my brain about what could have happened to my dear little charm and I suddenly remembered . . .' She headed unerringly for the armchair.

'I was sitting in this chair' – she suited her action to the words – 'and – oh!'

Pasha bounded into her lap with a glad cry of welcome. It was the only welcome she was getting, but it seemed to be enough for her.

'Oh, you beautiful, beautiful darling!' Vivien wrapped her arms around him and he nestled into the luxurious mohair purring happily.

Bettina was aware of a faint sound from the kitchen, as of the back door closing. Graeme must have thought this was a friend come to visit and decided to slip away quietly. She hoped he had remembered not to let Adolf out.

'Doesn't he look gorgeous against the dark green?' Vivien gazed down at Pasha, lost in admiration. Pasha raised his head to nuzzle her chin.

While they communed silently, Bettina quickly checked the kitchen. Graeme had gone but, thank heaven, Adolf was still there. He greeted her with a loud complaint.

'You stay with me.' She picked him up. 'I want to keep an eye on you.' She carried him back into the living room and took a seat on the sofa.

Adolf and Pasha exchanged complacent glances from the respective arms enfolding them. This was the life. This was the way it ought to be all the time.

'Isn't it nice to have such a beautiful day?' Vivien lowered Pasha to her lap and smiled nervously.

'Yes.' Bettina waited for the next move.

'You know, I had cats when I was a child. I'd almost forgotten how much I liked them.' Her hand, toying with Pasha's ears, seemed to be trembling. Pasha turned and gave her a curious look. 'I've been so busy in recent years, so caught up in my work, that I haven't had time to enjoy life properly.'

'Yes,' Bettina agreed. 'Market research must be quite arduous.'

'Mark—? Oh! Oh, yes!' Her smile wavered before she caught it and stretched her lips wide again. 'It is!'

Bettina smiled back serenely. Liars needed a good memory. Vivien was having increasing trouble keeping her story straight. Perhaps her mistake was mixing in bits of her genuine personal life; her story was unravelling at the edges – and so was she.

'Well, as I was saying' – Vivien attempted a recovery, speaking over-brightly and fumbling for her bag – 'I remembered sitting in this chair and feeling a . . . a sort of *tug* at my wrist when I got up to leave—'

Bettina forbore to point out that she had actually been sitting in the other armchair. It was Huntley Forrest who had been sitting in that one.

'And I thought . . . possibly . . . my charm might have caught on the plush and . . . and fallen . . .' Vivien began groping down between the armrest and the seat cushion.

Bettina watched quietly as Vivien clawed her way down to the frame of the chair with increasing panic.

'It's *got* to be here!' Vivien choked out. 'I . . . I mean, I was so sure. It *came* to me – almost like a revelation – that this was the only spot it *could* be . . .'

She leaped up, tumbling Pasha to the floor, and wrenched the seat cushion off the chair. And sneezed.

'Sorry about the dust,' Bettina said unrepentantly, as Vivien stared down at the denuded seat with hysterical incredulity. 'I'm afraid the housekeeping around here isn't all that it might be.'

'I don't understand . . .' Vivien began scrabbling at the lint bordering the base where the cushion had rested. 'It *has* to be here! There's no other place unless you've rearranged the furniture and I really sat in the other chair.'

'I haven't,' Bettina said calmly.

'Oh!' Vivien's face cleared. 'Here it is!' She pulled up a small flat object, showering dust and lint in its wake. 'I'm *so* pleased to have it again . . .' She blew on it to disperse the last of the dust – and suddenly her face was not pleased at all.

'This isn't my charm!' She glared down at it in furious dismay. 'This is a threepenny bit. An old threepenny bit!'

'Dear, dear,' Bettina said. 'Has it been that long since Mother vacuumed the chairs? I must mention it to her next time she tells me how hard she works at the house-keeping.'

'Oh!' Vivien hurled the offending coin across the room and advanced on the other armchair. 'Then it must be this one – it *has* to be!' She began dismembering the chair with increasing hysteria.

Pasha retreated to sit beside Bettina's ankles, looking worried. Adolf watched with detached interest and a certain amount of speculation; if she unearthed anything of real interest, like a mouse, he was more than ready to join in the game.

'I can't understand it . . .' Vivien tore at the chair. 'It *must* be here somewhere!'

'You seem very certain.' Bettina allowed a trace of scep-ticism to shade her tone. 'Yet you must have visited a lot of houses over the weekend.'

'Not that many. I mean— Yes, I did. But not many people were home.' She looked at Bettina in desperation. 'Perhaps the sofa . . .'

'Why don't you put the chair cushions back first,' Bet-tina suggested reasonably. 'This room is beginning to look as though burglars have been ransacking it.'

'Oh! Yes, sorry. I'm not usually so—' Vivien dived to replace the cushions; her sleek hairdo was falling to pieces. She ran her hand through it distractedly. 'He— *I* must have got muddled. I must have been sitting on the sofa after all.'

Bettina rose patiently to allow her to attack the sofa cushions. She was still standing when, distraught and on the verge of tears, Vivien finished her unsuccessful search and turned to face her again.

Perhaps something showed in her expression because Vivien suddenly looked wary.

'Is this—?' Bettina took the charm from her pocket and held it out. 'Is this what you're looking for?'

'Yes! That's it!' Vivien snatched at it. 'You let me go through all that – and you've had it all the time,' she accused. 'Why didn't you tell me? Where did you find it?'

'In the first armchair,' Bettina said. 'Right where your husband planted it. Huntley Forrest *is* your husband, isn't he?'

'Oh! Oh! You've known all along, haven't you?' Vivien burst into tears. 'Oh, I can't go on! I'm no good at this!'

'No, you're not,' Bettina said. 'Suppose you tell me what you've *really* lost.'

Vivien nodded, sobbing too heartily to speak for the moment. She sank down on the chair, hunched over, shaken by the force of her tears.

Pasha crept over to comfort her. She pulled him into her lap and clung to him, seeming to draw strength from him. Her sobs gradually diminished.

'My disks!' she choked out. 'All my hard disks are gone!'

CHAPTER 16

'Your *what?*' It was the last thing Bettina had expected to hear. It made no sense at all.

'My top-secret programme,' Vivien said. 'My life's work, practically. The last several years of my life, certainly. Gone, all gone! The software has disappeared.'

'I thought you just said hard—' Bettina stopped, aware of the half-pitying, half-superior look Vivien was giving her.

'You don't know anything about computers, do you?' Vivien asked.

'No,' Bettina said. 'But I gather you do.'

'Yes.' Vivien gave a deep sigh, a final dab at her nose and whisked her handkerchief back into her bag. 'I'm rather good with them, in fact.'

'And you have nothing to do with market research.' It was a flat statement, Bettina had had no doubt for a long time.

'Only in the larger sense.' Vivien smiled faintly. 'Our firm commissions it sometimes.'

That was a lot more believable. Bettina waited.

'Huntley and I have our own firm,' Vivien said. 'Basically, we devise computer programmes. We started out doing special projects for private clients, then we began working out general programmes for commercial sale. We've done rather well.' She toyed modestly with one of the other charms on her bracelet. It was now clear that it was meant to be a computer screen and not a television screen; Bettina remembered wondering about it.

'And we're planning to do even better. I've been

working on something rather unusual for the past few years. I won't say it's revolutionary – but it's pretty damn good. The trouble is, I wanted it to be perfect, so I've kept on tinkering with it and—' She broke off, suddenly intent on stroking Pasha.

'It's my fault. I kept everything in the computer. I didn't want to download until it was just right. I didn't—' After a quick glance at Bettina's face, she elucidated. 'I didn't take any copies of the programme. I didn't keep any outside records. I didn't have a backup. I left it all in the computer, except for the original – the one and only – set of hard disks. And they've been stolen. If I don't get them back, it's all gone.' She looked at Bettina sharply. 'Do you understand?'

'Not quite,' Bettina said honestly. 'But I'll take your word for it. What I really don't understand is why you keep coming back here. We haven't got your disks.' She had a momentary vision of the carrier pigeon fluttering lopsidedly through the storm, weighed down by a box of disks swinging from one leg. Where did the pigeon fit into this? Or did it?

'I—' Vivien looked at her earnestly, looked away, then looked back again. 'Oh, I *wish* I knew whether I could trust you!'

Strange, that's just what I've been thinking about you. They stared at each other silently. Bettina felt Adolf's tail tapping against her arm like a metronome.

The telephone shrilled abruptly, tearing into the silence, startling them both. Bettina was the first to recover.

'It's probably for you,' she said, going to answer it.

'Bettina?' Zoe's voice was strained and almost unrecognizable.

'Zoe! Where are you?'

'At the hospital . . .' Zoe took a deep ragged breath. 'My mother has just died.'

'Oh, Zoe. I'm so—'

'And yours has collapsed.' Zoe took another noisy

breath. 'I'm sorry, Bet. You'd better get over here right away.'

'Oh, no!' Suddenly dizzy, Bettina leaned against the wall, letting Adolf thud to the floor. He yelped a protest.

'What is it?' Vivien hurried into the hall. 'What's the matter?'

'My mother ... hospital ...' Bettina took a ragged breath of her own and spoke to Zoe. 'I'll be right there. As soon as I can get a taxi.'

'Don't be silly,' Vivien said. 'I'll drive you.'

'Thank you.' Bettina started for the door, then remembered. 'Oh! Adolf!' She looked round for him, found him crouched hopefully beside the front door, trying to look invisible, swooped and captured him.

'I'll just lock him up,' she told Vivien, 'and be right with you. Oh, you might bring Pasha. He can go in his carrier, too, then I shan't have to worry about what they're getting up to when I'm not here.'

'If you're worried about them.' Vivien picked up Pasha, who had stayed close to her side. 'I could come back and look after them until you get back. I wouldn't mind at all – and you wouldn't have to shut them up.'

'They'll be all right, they're used to it.' Bettina latched Adolf into his case. 'They're overdue for a nap, they'll just curl up and sleep until I get back.'

Adolf loosed a series of ear-splitting yowls, clearly calling her a liar and an unfeeling monster.

Pasha complained more softly; he didn't mind the carrying case but rightly suspected this meant he was about to be parted from his new friend again – and that really upset him. He tangled his claws in the mohair and protested sadly.

'Poor dears, they hate to be left alone,' Vivien said as Bettina disentangled Pasha and pushed him into his carrier.

'Where's Bluebell?' Bettina looked round for the missing member of the crew. She was nowhere to be seen.

'Oh, never mind.' It was more important to get to her

169

mother. Bluebell could be trusted not to get into too much mischief.

'I'll come back and look for her.' Vivien was obviously determined to be here and have the house to herself – for all the good it would do her. The diamonds were still in Bettina's pocket. There was nothing to be found in the house – unless Adolf misbehaved in his carrier. And Vivien did not strike Bettina as someone who would rush to clean up after Adolf. She would be far more likely to pretend she hadn't noticed it had happened and leave it for Bettina to clean up.

'It wouldn't be any trouble,' Vivien urged. 'And you don't know how long you might be gone. I can feed them and—'

'All right, if you insist.' It was easier to give in. Vivien was providing a lift to the hospital and would otherwise keep badgering her all the way.

'Just don't let Adolf out of his carrier, no matter how much he nags,' Bettina said, adding for good measure, 'He's been acting oddly lately and I'm afraid he might be coming down with something – and you wouldn't want Pasha to catch it.'

'Certainly not!' Vivien immediately moved Pasha's carrying case a good distance away from Adolf's. 'I'll see that he stays where he is.'

'When you're ready to leave,' Vivien said, drawing up in front of the hospital, 'just ring the house. I'll come and pick you up.'

'This has been very kind of you.' Bettina got out. 'But Zoe has her car here, I'll get a lift home with her.'

Just as Bettina was closing the door, a disquieting thought occurred to her. 'Vivien – be careful.'

'I've told you I won't let Adolf out.'

'No, I didn't mean that. I mean . . . Mrs Rome was alone in her house when she was attacked. And now you're going to be alone in our house . . . Be careful. Lock the doors.'

'I'll be all right,' Vivien said blithely. 'Don't worry. Lightning never strikes twice in the same place.'

'Yes, but this is the place next door.' But Vivien had gunned the motor and driven off.

Bettina looked after her unhappily. Should she have denied her access to the house? Too many inexplicable things were going on in the formerly quiet neighbourhood. Or was Vivien so deeply involved that she was perfectly safe?

And why had Graeme been prowling about in the back garden with that stupid excuse about a cat crying? Had he any reason to suspect that Sylvia had never left for Edinburgh at all? Did he think she might have been the first to encounter the man who had killed Mrs Rome? Was her body lying somewhere in the bushes awaiting discovery? But the police had gone over the area thoroughly when the workman's body had been found. Had that been the accident it seemed?

And why was she standing here outside the hospital asking herself all these questions? She knew the answer to that one: because it was easier than going through those doors to face whatever was awaiting her. She took a deep breath and started forward.

Then Zoe was coming to meet her. Zoe, with an expression on her face Bettina had never seen before.

'Sorry, Bettina,' Zoe said. 'She really did have a bad heart, after all.'

After the car had swerved for the third time, Bettina's nerve snapped, her mother's grim foreboding echoing at the back of her mind.

'Be careful! You almost hit that tree.' Perhaps it had been ill-considered to begin telling Zoe the story of the Bank Holiday weekend while she was driving.

'Sorry about that.' Zoe pulled over to the kerb. 'You now have my undivided attention. Keep talking.'

'Actually, that's about all there is to it.' Bettina found that she had run out of words. She didn't want Zoe's undivided attention; it was too much like a dress rehearsal for the talk she would have to have with Inspector Hughes. He seemed a pleasant, mild-mannered man, but the thought of his undivided attention suddenly terrified her.

'Oh, is *that* all?' Zoe was heavily sarcastic. 'Hardly worth bothering to mention, was it?'

'I haven't really had a chance to talk to you since you got back,' Bettina defended. 'Someone was always around.'

'Well, they won't be now,' Zoe said bleakly.

'No.' The tears were perilously close again. 'Do you— Do you think it was my fault? What happened to your mother? To my mother?'

'Not in the way you mean it,' Zoe said. 'I think you're the classic case of the innocent bystander, minding your own business and suddenly pitched into a situation not of your making which you couldn't begin to understand. The best thing to do was keep quiet. If you'd started shouting about it, you might have got us all killed. I mean—'

'They've been killed anyway.' Bettina stared blankly out of the window, she couldn't look at Zoe. Her hands suddenly felt very cold; she began rubbing them. Her feet were freezing, too.

'That's enough for now.' Zoe started the car again, took an unexpected turn and they rolled off in the opposite direction.

'Aren't we going home?'

'Not quite yet.' Zoe made another turn; the lights of a late-night shopping centre loomed ahead. 'We have one little errand to do first.'

When Zoe came out of the off-licence, she was carrying two clanking bags. 'Scotch, gin and brandy,' she announced. 'With a few mixers. That should see us through the night.'

'More than one night,' Bettina said.

'Oh, I don't know.' Zoe dumped her shopping in the

back. 'From what you've been telling me, I have the feeling we might have company.'

'That policewoman did say someone would be along to question us again.' Bettina felt almost proud of herself for being able to remember anything at this stage. 'Because it's a murder case now. But the police aren't allowed to drink on duty.' She looked at Zoe in sudden confusion. 'Are they?'

'You're not trying to confuse the issue,' Zoe assured her. 'You're just in a state of shock.'

Shock. Bettina closed her eyes and a wave of red seemed to pass across them. The red of the Romes' floor. But Zoe wouldn't have that much of a shock because Mother had gone in and thoughtfully cleaned up the kitchen. It was Mother who had had the worst shock – and it had killed her.

The murderer had killed both mothers – but the policewoman had said that Mrs Bilby wouldn't count, strictly speaking. The killer hadn't laid a finger on her. Indirect killing couldn't be prosecuted. No one could have known how weak Mrs Bilby's heart was – or how fatally her friend's death would affect her.

Someone gave a sob – and Bettina realized it was herself.

'Easy,' Zoe said. 'We're almost there.'

'Stay together!' Zoe said as Bettina veered off towards her own gate. 'We want to put the supplies in my house – and then I want to take a good look at that pigeon.'

'Adolf—'

'Forget about Adolf!' Zoe could say that. She didn't know. Bettina had not quite got round to explaining about Adolf and his appetite yet.

'The cats are safer than we are!' And that was no lie. 'Take one of these bags.'

Bettina complied and followed Zoe into the Rome house. It seemed strangely cold and empty. With a great deal of trepidation, she trailed Zoe into the kitchen.

Mrs Bilby had done a good job. Only someone who had seen the room in its original state could know how good.

Fortunately, Zoe had no idea. She hesitated in the doorway then, seeing nothing out of place, marched forward to deposit her bag on the kitchen table and began unloading it.

It took Bettina rather longer to move forward and join Zoe. A helpless, trancelike state seemed to have descended upon her. She could move and observe, perhaps even talk if the impetus were strong enough, but for all the reality she was feeling she might well be in the midst of an out-of-body experience.

Shock, of course. Shock was the answer to everything these days. Shock and stress. Heaven knew there had been plenty of stress over the past few days.

'Put the ginger ale and tonic in the fridge,' Zoe directed, dealing with her own problems by trying to convince herself that she was in command of the situation.

Bettina obeyed Zoe's orders. It was easier than arguing. And what was there to argue about? Like an automaton, she moved the contents of her bag onto the shelves of Zoe's refrigerator, recklessly shoving the other items aside to make room for the bottles. Surely, Zoe had overbought; but that was probably the measure of her shock.

Bettina felt a great longing for her own bed. To sink down into it, pull the pillow over her head – no! Not that! She straightened up, eyes wide, gasping for air, fighting for control. The simplest cliché was fraught with menace at this point. A pillow was only comforting when it could be tossed aside at will. The vision of it being pushed down relentlessly, blocking air passages . . . held tight by an unseen enemy . . .

'Bettina!' The exasperation was worthy of Mrs Bilby. 'Shut the fridge door and come over here.'

Bettina turned – and quailed. Zoe was brandishing a large knife with a long, broad, sharp serrated edge.

'Now . . .' Zoe set the knife down on the table. 'Sit down and let me see those diamonds!'

Numbly, Bettina reached into her pocket, brought out the cylinder and balanced it on the table between them.

Zoe reached for it, twisted off the cap and spilled out the diamonds in a bright glittering arrow across the table. After one dismissive glance, she ignored them to concentrate on the little cylinder.

'Handmade,' Zoe decided, examining it closely, turning it round and round. 'Beaten out thin like pewter work. You can see the little flat surfaces where the hammer has hit. They needed it as thin as possible to reduce the weight so that the bird could carry more gems.'

'Yes,' Bettina said faintly. That made sense. It was not something she had thought about; she had been too stunned by the sight of the diamonds themselves.

'It's just a shell, practically an eggshell.' Zoe frowned down at it. 'Far too light to hold anything else.'

'That's right.' Bettina nodded. Now that the extreme fragility of the cylinder had been pointed out, she could see it. She had not noticed it before. She still could not see that the fact added to the sum of their knowledge. It was not as if the craftsman had signed his work.

'That leaves the bird itself.' Zoe pushed back her chair and strode towards the larder. 'Let's see what that can tell us.'

'No more than the message tube,' Bettina said. 'I looked.'

'Ah!' Zoe said. 'But did you look *inside?*'

'Inside what?'

'Inside . . .' Zoe gestured over her shoulder to the knife on the table. '. . . inside the *bird*.'

'You can't do that!'

'Oh, I think I can.' Zoe's voice was muffled as she bent over the freezer chest, rummaging in its depths. 'That knife is specially made for cutting frozen food. It ought to be sharp enough.'

'I mean—' Bettina winced away as Zoe brought the frozen pigeon over and slammed it down on the table, tearing away the shroud of paper towels. It seemed to

175

have shrunk a bit and looked terribly forlorn. Once it had been somebody's pet.

Zoe seemed to feel it, too. She picked up the knife, then stood hovering over the pigeon irresolutely, not quite sure where to start. After a moment, she turned it over, beak down, but that wasn't a great improvement. Bits of frost glittered in the crevices of its feathers.

'But why do you want to do this?' Bettina grimaced with distaste. 'What are you looking for?'

'The bug, of course,' Zoe said. 'There has to be one.'

'Bug?' Bettina recoiled.

'Not that sort of bug,' Zoe said impatiently. 'The tracing sort. The kind you hide under the dashboard or somewhere on a car and it gives out a location signal so that you can follow it. How else do you think those people knew where to start looking?'

'You think someone got some kind of electronic device into the pigeon?' The idea made a certain sense. 'But how?'

'How do I know? Maybe they rammed it down his craw. Maybe they had a vet do it, the way they implant microchips in dogs or cats so that they can always be identified. All I know is I sure as hell wouldn't load up a bird with a fortune in diamonds and send it winging off into the night without making damn sure I knew I could keep track of it. Would you?'

'No,' Bettina said slowly. All sorts of odd happenings could be explained if that were the case. 'Then all those people running around after the storm weren't trying to unblock drains, they were looking for the pigeon's body. They knew it had been last heard from in this general area, but they couldn't pinpoint the exact location. There must have been electrical interference from the storm disrupting the signalling; they might have thought their bug had short-circuited or something. Then I hid the pigeon in the deepfreeze – and that would have cut off any signals being emitted.'

'Exactly.' Zoe half closed her eyes and chopped downwards with the knife. It rebounded off the carapace of ice and feathers.

'When the transmitter stopped signalling, they thought the pigeon had been brought down in the storm and perhaps been swept into a gutter blocking a drain. That was why they were probing all the drains, they were desperate to find it before it went into the sewer and was carried out to sea. They were just giving up when—' She broke off as she remembered what had set them all off again.

'They must have gone mad thinking they'd lost all those diamonds.' Zoe was following her own train of thought. She attacked the bird with a sawing motion now and distressing crunching noises began filling the air. She appeared to be making some headway.

'Put it back!' Bettina caught at Zoe's arm. 'Put it back in the freezer. Quickly!'

'What's the matter with you?' Zoe gave her a distracted look. 'I've almost—'

'When you took it out of the freezer before . . .' Bettina said. 'That's when they came back. It's still transmitting signals. They'll be able to pinpoint us if you keep it out any longer. Put it back!'

'What makes you think they'll still be around?' Zoe was reluctant to stop, the pigeon was almost cut in half.

'They've never gone very far away. And Vivien is in my house with the cats. I'm sure she's one of them.'

'Oh, very well.' Zoe seemed only half convinced. She picked up the pigeon and, still holding the knife, started for the larder. 'Perhaps I can put it inside the freezer and keep working on it. The insulated sides and the electric current ought to muffle any signals.'

'I wouldn't bother,' a man's voice said behind them. 'It's too late. I'm afraid you've been caught red-handed.'

'Graeme!' Bettina found that she was not really surprised. There had always been a little too much unexplained about Graeme Martin. Yes, and Sylvia, too.

Zoe glanced down at her hands where tiny red crystals were liquidizing, literally turning her red-handed.

'Just put the knife down on the floor,' Graeme said, 'and bring the bird back to the table.'

'If I do,' Zoe tried to bargain, 'will you put that gun away?'

'Ah, no. I'm afraid that isn't part of the deal.'

'Are we going to have a deal then?' Zoe looked cheered.

'Perhaps.' Graeme gestured with the gun. 'First, the knife. On the floor. Slowly. No sudden moves.'

Zoe crouched, not taking her gaze from his face, and set the knife down at her feet. He nodded.

'Now over to the table,' he directed. 'Put the bird down. Carefully. Not near the—' His voice changed, possessiveness and avarice colouring it. 'Not near *my* diamonds.'

'*Your* diamonds?' That *did* surprise Bettina; her mother had been so sure that the Martins were on the verge of bankruptcy. Was this another of Sylvia's get-rich-quick schemes, like the art collection and the plan to breed Pasha?

'Did you buy them in Brussels?' Not too legally, perhaps, especially if he had had to smuggle them into this country by way of the carrier pigeon.

'Brussels?' He looked startled for a moment, then gave a short, mirthless laugh. 'No, I earned them. Here. Don't worry, they're mine, all right.'

'Is the pigeon yours, too?' Zoe laid the bird gently on the table, well away from the gems.

'Only in the family sense,' Graeme said. 'It belongs – belonged – to Sylvia's father. Pigeons are his hobby.' He glanced at the bird. 'Pity you felt it necessary to mutilate the thing. We'll have to tell him it got thrown away. Can't let the old boy see it like that. Ah, well, he has a loft full of the dreary blighters. No accounting for taste.'

'I gather you found it useful,' Zoe said.

'I thought it might be,' Graeme admitted. 'The most difficult part of this sort of procedure is collecting the ransom. That's where they have the best chance of catching you. I read about the carrier pigeon method in an old American true crime book. It was tried a few times in the 1920s and '30s. Now I can see why it didn't catch on.' He looked down at the bird distastefully.

'Even then, the main problem was that the pigeons were too easily distracted and didn't always fly straight home. It must have been unnerving to have a certified cheque – encashable by anyone who found it – or a small roll of high-denomination banknotes flying around out there somewhere and have to wonder, for perhaps days, whether your bird had been blown off course and lost at sea or been killed by some bloody cat when it landed for food.'

'They didn't do it,' Bettina defended automatically. 'The bird was dead of a broken neck when they found it.'

'I thought modern technology had overcome that problem.' He ignored her protestations. 'I planted a directional signal in the bird before Alf delivered it to, er, the people who were going to pay the ransom in nice unidentifiable diamonds. The theory was promising, but the execution left something to be desired. However' – he advanced on the table – 'all's well that ends well – and here are my diamonds.' He frowned down at them. 'Is this all of them?'

It was the question Bettina had been dreading. It came so suddenly she could not check the telltale movement of her hand towards her pocket.

'All right.' Graeme had not missed it. 'Let's have the rest of them. Slowly. No sudden moves.' He was more on edge than he looked. What was he planning to do with them?

Bettina slowly drew the large round brilliant-cut diamond from her pocket and set it on the table beside the others. Then, even more slowly, she brought out the large pear-shaped stone.

'Is that all?' Graeme was still suspicious. How much did he know?

'That's all,' Bettina said firmly. She could not let him know about Adolf. He had no feeling for cats at the best of times and poor Adolf wouldn't stand a chance against this man's greed.

'I'll just make sure of that.' Graeme moved in closer. 'Keep your hands up.' The gun was unnervingly pushed against her throat, tilted up towards her chin. Graeme groped in her pocket, bringing out and discarding with disgust the crumpled paper handkerchief.

'Don't hurt her,' Zoe pleaded.

'I have no intention of hurting anyone.' Graeme checked Bettina's other pocket and stepped back.

'Nice try.' He grinned at her cheekily. 'A little bit of larceny in every soul, eh?'

'It wasn't that.' Bettina felt herself flushing. 'They wouldn't fit back in the cylinder, that's all.' Indignantly, she wondered how she had suddenly been put in the wrong when it was Graeme who—

'I notice you kept the two largest ones.' Graeme gathered up the diamonds from the table and transferred them to one of his own pockets. 'Just get a bag for that damned pigeon,' he said to Zoe. 'I'll take it along with me and dispose of it.'

As long as that was all he disposed of. He was being terribly free with his information – as though it didn't matter how much they knew. Bettina met Zoe's worried eyes and realized that she was thinking the same thing.

'What happened to Sylvia?' Bettina demanded abruptly.

'Nothing, so far as I know,' Graeme said. 'She's moved back in with her father for the time being. His house is just a couple of miles from here, as the crow flies – and the pigeon ought to have flown. I think the old boy is still hoping his precious bird will flutter into the loft, as originally planned. Sylvia will be doing her best to smooth the old boy's ruffled feathers, but I'm afraid he'll never loan us one of his pigeons again. Ah, well, we're not likely to need one again.'

'Then Sylvia never went to Edinburgh? She never intended to go to Edinburgh? She's in this with you?'

'All the way. She's the one who set it up so that we would disappear from here with no questions asked.' Again he grinned at Bettina. 'You wouldn't be surprised, would you, if I moved out after discovering that my loving wife had run away with another man, having first blackened my name all over the neighbourhood? The house is far too big for me to manage on my own – quite apart from the unhappy memories it holds.'

'It might have worked,' Bettina said slowly. 'Except that now we know all about it.'

'Sh!' Zoe hissed sharply, looking agonized.

'Ah, but who would believe you?' Graeme looked from one to the other. 'Without the diamonds and the pigeon, you have no evidence. It would simply be my word against yours. And you, forgive me, are two ladies of a Certain Age, who have recently suffered a great shock and may have lost control over your imaginations.'

'You'd never get away with that!' Zoe was stung into tactlessness herself.

'On the other hand,' he said cheerfully, 'I might tell everyone that you had made unwelcome advances to me, either separately or together, and were now taking revenge by lying about me because I spurned your fair bodies. Yes, that would be better. People are always willing to believe the worst about their neighbours. You'd be a laughing stock – and you wouldn't like that, would you?'

Shocked into silence, Bettina realized that he might

effectively have silenced them permanently – and blood-lessly. Even though their friends would never believe such a thing of them, some mud must stick and there would be a lifetime of hidden jeers, jokes and sidelong glances.

'I knew you'd take my point.' Graeme smiled at the expression on her face. 'So this will be our little secret, won't it?'

Zoe slapped a plastic bag down on the table with a con-trolled fury that betrayed her helplessness.

'What about the victim?' Bettina said. 'Can you guaran-tee silence there, too?'

'Victim?' Graeme looked honestly amazed. 'What victim?'

'The kidnap victim. You said the diamonds were a ransom.'

'No, no!' Graeme was injured. 'How could you think such a thing? Don't you know this is the Technological Age? All I "kidnapped" was a bit of equipment. The owners have come up with the ransom and I'll return their property now. No fuss, no muss, no bother. It was the perfect crime: a victimless crime.'

'Victimless!' The back door had opened silently and Vivien Smythe-Forrest stood in the doorway like an avenging angel. 'What about me? My work! Where is it?'

'Vivien!' Graeme shrank back. 'What are you doing here? How did you find this place?'

'We planted a signalling device in the bird, of course,' Vivien said. 'Did you really imagine we'd load it with dia-monds and send it off into the blue without trying to keep in contact in some way?'

Zoe met Bettina's eye and nodded – just what *she* had said. And that, Bettina realized, was why Huntley Forrest had asked to use the telephone. What she had taken to be a mobile phone had really been the frequency detector for the bug they had planted in the pigeon.

Bettina spared a moment of pity for the pigeon. Two directional signalling devices inside him and a cylinder of diamonds on his leg! It was surprising that the poor bird had been able to take to the sky at all, less so that he had had trouble staying airborne.

'You little swine!' Vivien's fury impelled her forward. 'To think I trusted you! Made you my assistant!'

'No, stay there!' Graeme remembered his gun and waved it at her. 'Don't come any closer.'

'I wouldn't want to get any closer to you! I couldn't believe anyone I knew would have done such a thing to me. Not until I saw you outside this house last night. Then I knew something was wrong. This isn't the address we have for you on our records.'

'The address you have is correct,' Graeme said. 'We just had to rent it out because of negative equity problems. We've been camping out in the house over here for the past couple of years.'

'I don't care about that!' Vivien advanced into the room. She did not appear to notice that Pasha had followed her and was close by her feet. 'Where are my disks? Where is my programme?'

'In the house,' Graeme said.

'Which house?' Vivien snapped.

'Number twenty-seven – the best in the road.' Graeme grinned. 'Sylvia insisted on it. Since you've paid the ransom . . .' He tossed a key on the table. '. . . there you are. You can go in and pick them up right now, if you like. You'll find everything in the top drawer of the dressing table in the master bedroom. Don't worry about returning the key. I won't be going back there.

'And . . .' He hesitated momentarily. '. . . I suppose you can consider this my resignation.'

'You're fired!' Vivien snapped. 'Retroactively. You were fired the moment you took those disks. Huntley will settle the score with you later.'

'Oh, come now.' Graeme seemed amused rather than worried by the threat. 'You've got your disks back. And you know you'll manage to claim the money for the ransom back from the insurance company – one way or another. You haven't been harmed at all.'

183

'Unlike my mother,' Zoe said quietly.

'And mine,' Bettina added.

'No! No, I had nothing to do with that.' Graeme frowned uneasily, his self-image as benevolent Master Criminal wavering. 'You said so yourself. Some intruder broke in.'

'The only intruders in this neighbourhood were looking for that pigeon,' Bettina said. 'You're responsible for it being here – and that makes you responsible for the intruders. The alleged workmen. Who were they – your backup team?'

'I had nothing to do with them,' Graeme said quickly. 'This may be the Technological Age, but there are still a lot of Neanderthals around – and leave it to my father-in-law to find them. They're *his* friends. We needed someone who wouldn't be recognized to deliver the pigeon to Viv and Hunt. Sylvia's father volunteered his friends. We didn't tell them anything, but Alf and Len knew something was going on. They hung around and, when the pigeon was released, they followed it in the van by visual sighting with binoculars. Obviously, they hoped that it would make a landing before it reached home and they could get a look at what it carried. They were pretty sure it must be something valuable – and they were curious.'

'They were also violent,' Bettina said. 'I don't believe that man in the puddle died accidentally. I'd seen them quarrelling several times. What happened? Thieves falling out?'

'I haven't got to the bottom of that yet,' Graeme said. 'They both had filthy tempers, especially Alf – the survivor. A real nasty bit of work. I wouldn't put it past him to have bashed Len over the head with something if they had any kind of disagreement. The fact that they were both wet and cold and miserable would only have made his temper worse. Alf is a right bullyboy – I wouldn't have trusted him an inch myself. If he started to question anyone and didn't like the answers he was getting – or wasn't getting, he—' Graeme broke off, suddenly realizing how much he was admitting he knew – or suspected.

'Trust!' Vivien spat. '*You* talk about trust! That's rich!'

Pasha moved out from behind her ankles and also spat at Graeme. If Vivien wanted a cat fight with Graeme, he was on her side. He'd always known Graeme was a rotter and his friend was showing her impeccable taste by hating him too.

'Oh, God! That beast again!' Graeme's foot drew back.

'Don't you dare!' Vivien snapped.

'Having trouble?' a voice inquired smoothly from the back doorway.

Everyone froze into a silent tableau.

'Or should I say, "Evening, all"?' Inspector Hughes strolled into the room, looking around with interest.

'Inspector Hughes,' Bettina said thankfully. 'How nice to see you.'

'Wonderful!' Zoe agreed enthusiastically.

'Come in, come in.' Graeme waved him in expansively. Somehow the gun had disappeared from his hand.

'Anything wrong?' Inspector Hughes had assessed the atmosphere expertly. He looked from one to the other, seeking clarification.

'No, no, I was just leaving. The ladies—' – Graeme leered at them – 'were just trying to press me to stay and join in a little orgy, but I promised them "another time".'

'You must excuse Graeme,' Zoe said sullenly. 'He has a rotten sense of humour.'

'Terrible.' Bettina also caved in under the implied threat. Inspector Hughes was the last person in the world she wanted to have a bad opinion of her.

'Then I'll say goodnight.' Graeme started for the front door.

'What about Pasha?' Zoe asked. Hearing his name, Pasha came forward and spat at Graeme again.

'As far as I'm concerned' – Graeme looked down at the cat viciously – 'you can strangle the little sod and dump him in the nearest river!'

Pasha spat again – that went double in spades for him.

'You don't want him?' Vivien asked incredulously.

'Hell, no! If you do' – Graeme looked at her speculatively – 'take him. You're welcome to him. A little bonus for a nice little girl. A nice *quiet* little girl.'

'Come to Mummy, darling!' Vivien swooped and picked up Pasha, setting him on the table and fussing over him. Somehow, the key to Graeme's house disappeared from the table.

'But he's not your cat,' Zoe protested. 'He's Sylvia's.'

'Believe me, she doesn't want him now. Besides, we're going to be doing a lot of travelling. Good luck, Viv. Just don't try to breed him,' Graeme added with a snigger. 'He's not as good as he looks.'

'Neither are you!' Vivien retorted, but her only answer was the slam of the front door.

'Care to tell me what's going on?' Inspector Hughes seemed to ask without a great deal of hope.

'Not right now,' Zoe said. 'I told you we'd have company, Bettina. Let's break out those bottles.'

'Yes, but—' Bettina looked at Inspector Hughes. 'Are you on duty? The policewoman said you'd be around with more questions.'

'Not tonight,' he said. 'I've heard about your mother. This is just a private condolence call.'

'In that case' – Bettina gathered up the bottles – 'let's move next door to my place.' She looked at the spot on the floor where they had found Mrs Rome, then looked at Inspector Hughes. 'Please.'

'Let me help you with those bottles,' he said gallantly.

They were relaxing in the living room with their drinks. Vivien, with a self-mocking grimace at Bettina, had reclaimed the armchair she had been so interested in earlier. Inspector Hughes was in the other armchair, still watchful and wary, straining to interpret the nuances of the conversation.

Bettina and Zoe were on the sofa. The cats, having been invited to join in the drinks, were clustered round a large soup bowl filled with cod-liver oil.

'My mother used to tell me, "Some day all will be explained,"' Inspector Hughes said. 'I hope she was right.'

'Perhaps' – Zoe glanced at her watch – 'in about another twenty-four hours. Or forty-eight,' she added for good measure.

'There's no evidence, of course,' Vivien said. She had excused herself earlier on the pretext of getting something from her car. From the smug expression on her face when she returned, Bettina knew that the treasured hard disks were safely in the depths of her shoulder bag. 'And no one will press charges. That's the trouble with computer crimes: the computer companies don't dare admit how easily they can be taken. It has to be hushed up.'

'Doubtless some accommodation could be made.' Inspector Hughes stretched out his legs casually, only the faint tautness of his jaw suggesting that this was the first he had heard about computers. 'But it's up to the Crown to press charges in a murder case.'

'Yes,' Zoe said grimly. 'We'll want that to go ahead. But it doesn't directly involve Gr—'

'Let me freshen your drinks!' Bettina jumped up noisily, making a great production of it. 'And the cats shall have more cod-liver oil, too. Oh—' She upended the bottle over the soup bowl. 'Oh, that's all there is. Pasha is fresh out of cod-liver oil.'

'I'll get more in the morning,' Vivien said. 'I'll get a gallon jug. He shall have all he wants.'

'That isn't a good idea,' Inspector Hughes said mildly. 'Cod-liver oil is the kind of treat that should be strictly rationed. For his own good.'

'Oh, but he loves it so.'

'Yes, but it doesn't love him.' Inspector Hughes looked rather uncomfortable, his ears went red at the edges. 'You mustn't give a cat too much cod-liver oil. An overdose of Vitamin A can render them sterile. We had a case at the local cat club—'

'*What?*' Bettina and Zoe looked at each other.

'As soon as she stopped overdosing the cat with cod-liver oil, he reverted to normal in just a few—' He stopped, drowned out by the shrieks of laughter.

'Oh, wait till Sylvia hears this!' Bettina gasped. 'It will *kill* her!'

'I hope so!' Zoe whooped. 'I *hope* so!'

Inspector Hughes stayed behind after the others had left. Bettina tried to convince herself that it wasn't because he considered her the weakest link in the chain of silence.

Adolf sat happily in front of the fire; the other cats had been carried away and he now reigned as Only Cat, a situation completely to his liking. Bettina was glad that he was willing to settle down where she could keep an eye on him. She had checked his cage when she let him out and it was pristine. How long could he hold out? Or hold on?

The hour was late, the drinks were strong, the company was congenial – and Inspector Hughes was a very sneaky questioner.

Bettina found herself telling him the story.

'I don't really see that there's much the police can do about it,' she finished. 'Although it seems a shame to let Graeme and Sylvia get away with it, even if the Forrests won't testify.'

'It sounds as though the Martins will be out of the country by now, but they'll be back eventually. The murders are more important and, even though it might be argued that the Martins are morally responsible, the law will settle for the actual perpetrator. Alf sounds as though he has form and it shouldn't take long to nail him. The autopsy report on his friend, Len, shows that he not only received a severe blow to the head, but there's mud and bruising to suggest a foot placed on the back of his neck to hold him face down in the water until he died. We'll collect Alf's footwear and turn Forensics loose on it. There should be enough for a conviction on that charge and they'll probably find traces of blood from Mrs Rome—' He broke off as Bettina shuddered against him.

188

'It's so awful,' she said.

'Have another drink . . .' He plied her with liquor expertly and went back to the less emotive subject.

'As for Graeme and Sylvia Martin, with no one willing to press charges or testify and with no hard evidence . . .'

'Hard disks . . .' He must have judged the amount correctly, for she giggled.

'And no diamonds . . .'

'Oh, there's one diamond left.' She giggled again. 'A nice, big emerald-cut diamond.'

'What?' Inspector Hughes sat up straight, sending her flying. 'There's a piece of real evidence? Good girl! We might be able to do something if you've still got a diamond up your sleeve.'

'Ummm . . . well . . .' She gave Adolf a long thoughtful look. Adolf stared inscrutably back at her.

'It's not exactly . . . up my sleeve,' she said.